Dedication

I want to dedicate this book to you my readers! You took the leap of faith with my first book and then you have responded to Tasha's story with such great emotion. I have been touched by some of the messages that I have received from my readers telling me about their experience as an abuse victim. You are all so strong, thank you for trusting me with your story!

I hope you all enjoy the conclusion to Tasha's story, this isn't goodbye so watch out for them in the near future!

I thank you all for trusting me on this emotional rollercoaster and I look forward to welcoming you on future journeys.

Prologue

I hear someone screaming, I realise it's me. What is Felix doing to me now? Why does he have to keep torturing me? I thought he loved me!

All of a sudden I can hear my name being called repeatedly, "Tasha, Tasha, are you ok?" I look around to see who is talking and then I look at my phone and realise that Luca has answered my call.

"L..L...Luca. F...F...Felix," I can't talk, I can't believe what Felix has done this time. "L...L...Luca. Ring Dad. Come quick, please." I'm sobbing, I'm not sure he can understand me.

"Tasha, where are you? What is going on? I can't hear you very well, why are you whispering?" he says.

"F...F...Felix, Luca come quick please. Home – I'm at home."

"Oh my God Tasha what has he done to you this time, I'll fucking kill him. Stay hidden and I'll be there as soon as I can. I'll ring your dad and ask him to meet me there. Love you Tasha." He hangs up. I stay where I am, curled into a little ball, rocking backwards and forwards.

I can't believe Felix has done this to me, this is the last straw, I can finally feel myself losing it, I've had enough, I can't deal with this any longer.

1

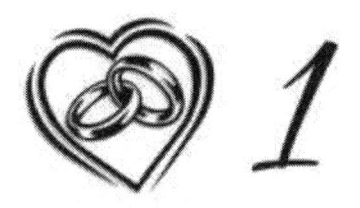

I don't know how long I sit there just rocking, but soon the front door opens and my Dad storms in, his eyes are darting all around the place looking for me, searching. When he sees me he runs towards me and takes me into his arms. "Baby girl, what happened, I'll kill him, I really will," he is still looking around, searching for Felix. I can't talk, I am so happy to see Dad.

Luca storms in the door then and his eyes land on me, he comes over to me and checks me over. "Tasha are you ok? What happened babe?" he's looking around himself too, taking in the mess of the trashed lounge.

"F...F...Felix, L...L...Luca he's upstairs." I can't even look towards the stairs.

Luca looks at me and then slowly walks to the bottom of the stairs, I think he knows what Felix has done, he can't bring himself to walk any faster to get to the stairs. He looks up and sees Felix, he is hanging from the attic doorway. "Oh no, Felix what have you done?" he runs up the stairs, but I know it's too late, it was already too late when I walked into the house.

Dad looks at me and says, "Are you ok, I need to go to Luca." He kisses me on the head when I nod to say that it's fine. He stands and goes up the stairs two at a time.

I can hear Luca and Dad talking to Felix, trying to find out if it's too late or not. I know he is gone, I can feel it in my heart.

I can hear some shuffling of furniture and then I hear a thud, oh my god did they just take him down? I stand up and walk to the bottom of the stairs, I can see Felix he is still there staring down at me. Dad sees me and comes down the stairs, he picks me up and takes me to the kitchen, he puts me down on the table, then he searches the cupboard and finds a bottle of whiskey, he pours me a glass and makes me drink it. "You've had a bad shock." I do as he tells me because I feel really faint. He gives me another shot of the whiskey.

I can hear Luca moving around and talking to someone on the phone. "Dad, why would he do that to himself? He had his whole life ahead of him. He knew I was coming over! Do you think he did it on purpose so that I would find him? That's just sick." I sob into my Dad's belly as he hugs me.

"Baby girl, he was obviously still sick, Luca was telling me he wouldn't let him in the house since he came home." We sit there for what seems like hours until someone knocks on the front door, it's the ambulance men and the police. That's who Luca must have been calling. They get to work getting Felix down and they take him out to the ambulance in a black bag.

I run out of the house to the ambulance, I undo the zip and look at Felix I kiss him on the lips. I hate him and love him at the same time. How could he do this to himself? To me? I start thumping him on the chest telling him how selfish he was. They move me out of the way and close the doors to the ambulance. I turn around and the police are waiting for me, we all go in and sit around the dinner table. They ask lots of questions which we all answer, who is his next of kin? We explain what happened over the last few months, they say that it was obviously a suicide but there was no note.

They agree to talk to his parents, I hadn't really thought about them during this whole time, they never once contacted me to apologise for what he had done to me, but I know I must talk to them later. After what seems like days the police go, I lean into

Dad who cradles me like a baby. Luca stands up and starts pacing the floor. "Tasha I'm really sorry you had to see that. Felix was a bastard for doing that and everything else to you."

I stand up and go to him and hug him tight. "Felix was very lucky to have a good friend like you who stuck by him even though you didn't agree with what he had done. Thank you Luca for being there for him." He hugs me back, he doesn't need to say anything.

Dad says to both of us, "I've rung Mum and Kammie and they are waiting at the house for us all, Luca that includes you too son." Luca nods at my dad and leaves to go to my house. I'm not able to drive so I lock the house and leave my car behind and jump in with Dad.

When we get to the house, we go in and Mum flies at me and Dad and Kammie flies to Luca. I can hear him crying into her neck, she is telling him it will be alright and she will be there for him always. I can't cry anymore I've already cried so much, Mum is crying though, she can't believe he would do something like that.

We all sit down and drink whiskey, for the shock, and we talk about Felix, the old Felix and what a wonderful man he was. We tell funny stories and laugh and then I remember that I need to speak to his Mum. I go into the kitchen and ring her. "Hi Barbara it's Tasha I'm so sorry about Felix."

"You have some nerve ringing this house, you drove him to this by telling him you were going to leave him when he was sick. You were supposed to protect him and look after him, not run at the first sign of him being sick." I can't believe her attacking me like that.

"What?! You obviously don't know why he was in hospital sick, he was a sick bastard towards the end." I'm shaking and I'm screaming into the phone.

I feel someone take the phone off me and it's Luca, "Barbara I'm sorry about Felix, but he did some terrible things to Tasha that's why she said those things." He walks out into the garden, obviously to tell her what he has done over the last month or so.

Kammie comes in and hugs me and takes me back to the lounge. I can't believe what a shit life I have right now. Luca comes back in and says that Barbara didn't have a clue what Felix had been doing to me and she apologised for shouting at me and also for what her son had done. I've always got on with her so it was a shock to hear her lose it like that. I know she was in shock at hearing the news about Felix hanging himself.

I know that I will have to go and see her before the funeral, but that isn't something I want to think about right now, I need to have a good night's sleep first.

Luca and Kammie stay over, Kammie climbs into bed with me and Luca stays in the spare room. I told her she could go to him but she said he would be ok and she can take care of him tomorrow, but tonight I needed her more. She really is the best friend in the world.

2

Surprisingly, I sleep well but that must have been the whiskey. I think of all the things that need to be done and get up and go downstairs. Kammie is still asleep; she looks so peaceful so I don't wake her. Mum is in the kitchen with the coffee machine on, "Do you want a cup baby girl?" I nod.

"Mum, I want to write a list of everything that needs to be done for the funeral and then afterwards. Will you help me?" I sit at the kitchen table.

"Of course I will baby girl, but don't you think you need to rest today and let us do the organising?" she says.

"No I need to do this; I need to know he's really gone. I still can't believe it Mum." I have a few tears fall down my cheek, but I wipe them away and get out my laptop and turn it on. Mum passes me a cup of coffee and then I start a list of things to do:

- Ring the funeral home
- Ring the church to arrange the funeral
- Decide where to have the "afters"
- Look at which picture to use for the memorial cards
- Where to post the obituary

When I've finalised the list I get up from the table and take a walk in the garden, I just need to think for a while. I sit on the bench and think about the last few years and all the things that have happened, I think about my wedding day and what a wonderful day it was. I was so in love that day, nothing could spoil the day, we ate, we laughed, we danced, and we made love all night. I can't help but think of the last time we were alone together and everything he put me through, I try to push it out of my mind, to think of all the good things we did, all the good times we had, and that's how I want to remember him.

When I walk back into the kitchen I'm surprised to see Caleb talking to my Mum. What is he doing here? Why is he talking to my Mum?

"Hi Caleb, what's going on?" I say as I close the door behind me.

"Tasha, I was worried because I hadn't heard from you, so I came over to see if you were ok. I couldn't sleep, I just felt like something was wrong and I needed to know that you were ok. You've been through so much lately." He walks over to me and pulls me into him and hugs me tight, he whispers in my ear, "Are you ok? I was so worried, I had a pain in my chest and I knew you were hurting. I'm so sorry Tasha, so sorry."

I pull back, "Thanks Caleb, I appreciate you coming over to see me, I'm fine, I just have a lot of things to organise now. I'll see you soon ok." I can't have him here, I can't think about him, I need to think about Felix and all the things I need to do to say goodbye. I take his hand and walk him to the front door, "Caleb you shouldn't have come here, I know you worry about me but honestly I'm fine."

"Tasha, you don't fool me, I know you're hurting and that's fine, but I want to help you in any way I can." He's trying to pull me in for a hug but I resist, I don't need this right now. I know that if he hugs me again, I won't want him to stop and I'll break down and I don't want to do that. Not in front of him!

"Ok, I'm going, but I will be here for you

and I will make sure you are ok because I worry about you. You can't push me away, I always protect those I care about Tasha." He kisses me on the cheek, walks through the door and gets in his car. I stand and lean against the wall breathing slowly to try and still my heart which is going mad.

I walk back into the kitchen, "Mum, why did you let him in?"

"He's your friend, you told me that when I asked you about him before." she says.

"I know I'm sorry, I was just surprised to find him here that's all. Mum, I need to ring work and tell them that I won't be back in this week, I think I'm going to tell them that I won't be back at all and just have time on my own before starting my new job." I know I should tell Mum that my new job is working for Caleb, but I just don't want to have to explain everything right now.

"Do you think that's the right thing to do Tasha? Shouldn't you be with other people instead of hiding away from the world?" She says coming over to me and rubbing my shoulder.

"I wouldn't be going to work this week anyway after what happened and then there's only two weeks left anyway, it's best if I don't go back because they all know Felix and I don't want to be reminded of us working together." I know it doesn't make sense, but it does to me.

"Ok honey, you go off and ring them and I will make you some breakfast." she says as she walks back into the kitchen.

I ring work and then go back into the kitchen and sit down. Work said that they understood and gave me their sympathies and that they were thinking of me. If I needed anything then I should ring them.

Kammie and Luca come down and join us for breakfast, they both have to go to work today and so they leave after they've eaten. I am so grateful for the two of them and when they leave I go with them to the door, "Guys, I don't know what I would have done without the two of you, Kammie you are the best friend anyone could ever want, thank you so much for being my friend." I kiss her on the cheek and hug her. "Luca, I don't know where to start, you are an amazing person, you stuck with Felix and protected me at the same time, I love you and hope that we will be friends for life." I kiss him and hug him too. I can feel tears coming to my eyes because I know I mean every word.

When they've left I go back to the kitchen and get another cup of coffee and then I make a start on the list and by lunchtime everything is organised for two days' time. "Mum, will you come with me to see Barbara and talk to them, they must be hurting right now too, and I have to remember that he belonged to them too."

"Of course I will baby girl, whatever you want to do, I'll be there."

We get dressed and drive over to Felix's parent's house, I knock on the door and they let us in. It is a bit awkward because of the abuse Barbara gave me on the phone, but I love them, they have been a part of my life for the last few years. Barbara apologises for losing it on the phone, she explains that she was in shock, which I can understand because I was in shock too.

We talk about the good times that we all had with Felix, much like we did the night before. "I'm going to the funeral home to see Felix on my way home, will you come with me Barbara, just to say goodbye. They have laid him out in the chapel of rest so we can go and see him." I ask because she needs to say goodbye too.

"I'd love that Tasha, come on let's go." she says to Bob. We drive over to the funeral home in two cars, so that we can go our separate ways after we've said goodbye. I'm nervous but I know I need to do this.

When we walk into the funeral home, we are met by Mr Walker who takes us to the chapel of rest; he offers his condolences to us all. Me, Bob and Barbara go into the chapel to see Felix, she goes straight up to the casket and starts to cry, Bob follows her and pulls her into a hug. I don't think I've ever seen him be demonstrative to her and I find it heartwarming, but heartbreaking at the same time. I can't go and see him yet so I stand with my back to the wall and just watch them. She's talking to him and telling how much she loves him and how much she will miss him. Bob is standing next to her holding her hand and just looking down into the coffin, he reaches out and touches Felix's hand and says, "Son, we are going to miss you so much, why did you have to do this? We would have helped you with anything, we love you." It's heartbreaking to watch, I take a couple of steps forward and touch Barbara on the shoulder, she turns and I take her in my arms, she sobs so hard I can feel her body shaking.

After a couple of minutes she calms down and says her final goodbye to Felix, she takes my hand and then they both walk out of the door, leaving me in the room with Felix on my own. I take one step at a time towards the casket until I'm right beside it, I slowly look inside and see Felix, he looks like he is asleep. I lean forward to see if he is breathing and it's all one of his big jokes, but he isn't. I put my hand on top of his and I talk to him and tell him I love him and I'll miss him, because I will, I don't think about the last month, I think about the rest of the time we had together. I brought our wedding rings with me and I put his on his finger and then I put mine on his little finger so that he has a part of me with him.

"To death us do part." I say to him while

I do it, I never thought that these vows would come true so soon. I lean over and kiss him on the lips, he feels so cold, so unlike Felix, but I know it is him and I feel a tear drip from my face onto his. "Goodbye Felix I love you, thank you for being a part of my life." I turn and walk out of the room and I don't look back.

After I have closed the door, I fall into my Mum's arms and sob. She walks me out of the home and into the car, she drives me home and we don't talk the whole way home. I just want this week to be over!

3

Dad is waiting for us when we get home, he has cooked dinner for us but I don't want any food, but I can't tell him. We sit at the table and Mum does all the talking, I just don't have the energy. "I think I'm going to go to bed, it's been a tough day." I say when dinner is finished, I just want to be on my own. I kiss Mum and Dad and then go upstairs; I undress and then fall into bed. I'm asleep within minutes and I sleep well, no bad dreams, no nightmares.

The following day goes past so fast, people are ringing to offer their condolences, they're popping into the house to see how I'm doing, and before I know it it's the day of the funeral. I wake up early and go down to the kitchen, I think I need a coffee to get me started; I put a tot of whiskey in it to help me through the day. The funeral car turns up half an hour before the funeral; I have dressed in a black dress and put my jacket on as its cold outside. When we get to the church, we wait outside for Felix's brother, my Dad, Felix's Dad, Luca and two other friends to carry his casket inside. It is really emotional, everyone is crying, I follow the casket down the aisle and think about the last time that I walked down this aisle was with Felix too, but under totally different circumstances.

The service is superb and then Luca stands up and talks about his life with Felix and how much of a loss it is. It is so emotional; I find it hard to breathe. I know it is my turn next, so I take a deep breath and walk to the podium.

"Thank you all for coming, the last time we were all together was under happier circumstances and none of us knew that we would be here a few short months later. Felix was a wonderful man, he was generous, loving, and had a heart of gold. It will be a great loss to each and every one of us here today to say our goodbyes to Felix." I can't say anything more, I certainly wasn't going to mention anything of the last couple of months, no one needs to know about that.

As I walk back to my seat on the front row I spot Caleb a couple of rows behind me, he smiles at me and I smile back. I can't believe he has come along to support me today; he is becoming a rock in my life.

The pallbearers carry the casket out to the grave and the priest says his final prayer as Felix is slowly lowered into the deep, dark, wet hole in the ground. I can't help crying out and I can feel myself getting weak, as I feel myself drifting closer to the ground I feel strong arms around me holding me up. I know whose arms they are and I realise that I need them around me, because I am not able to stand. I lean back into him and close my eyes. When I open them again, I see people are starting to leave the grave and walking back to their cars. I stand up straight and move away, I turn and say thank you to Caleb, he nods his head and follows me back to the funeral car. "I'm here for you Tasha don't forget that." he says.

"Thank you for coming Caleb it means a lot to me because I know you are only here for me and not for Felix." I get into the car and close the door, Mum and Dad are already in the car. I watch Caleb as his car drives away.

"That was nice of him to come Tasha, he did that for you, you know how he feels about Felix." I nod. I feel like an emotional wreck today. The driver takes us back to my house, where we have organised food and drinks for everyone. Kammie and Luca have cleaned the house up and fixed anything that was broken so that no one would know what had been going on in the house. I'm not sure how I feel about being back in this house and I'm not sure I want to move back in, but I will deal with that when I have to.

After a couple of hours people start to leave and then it is just me, Kammie, Luca, Mum, Dad and Felix's parents left. "Tasha we don't want you to be a stranger, you are a part of our family and we want you to stay that way. We love you like our own daughter and we don't want to lose touch." Barbara says and hugs me before she leaves as well.

I flop down on the couch and everyone else does the same. "How did you two manage to clean this house up so well in such a short space of time." I ask, because they really turned this house around.

They both look at each other like they don't want to say, "Well we had some help Tasha, we weren't going to say anything, but your friend Caleb helped us. When we left here the other day Kammie ran into him and he asked if there was anything he could do to help you, so we asked him to help us clean up your house as we knew you would want to come here after the service. He helped us a lot, he rolled up his sleeves and got his hands dirty. Tasha he's a very good friend you know."

I smile because I know he will do anything to help me, "I know Luca, I know."

"He also told us that your new job is working for his company, why didn't you tell us Tasha?" Kammie asks me.

"I didn't want anyone to think that I got the job because of him, I told him I wasn't going to take the job because I wanted to get the job on my own right, he said that I had already got the job before he became involved with the interviewing so I took the job. I was going to tell you all, but the moment never happened." I feel really guilty now.

"Tasha we all know that you are good at your job and what you do, no one would think that you got the job for any other reason than being the best candidate." Mum says.

I smile at them all, "I love you guys do you know that?"

We all laugh and then we talk about the service and the rest of the day, then Luca and Kammie leave and go home. Dad drives us back home because I don't want to stay in my house on my own, until I decide what I want to do with the house.

When I go to bed I take out my phone and ring Caleb, "Hey how are you?" I ask him when he answers.

"I think I'm supposed to be asking you that Tasha." he says.

"I'm fine, it was a hard day, which was to be expected really."

"I'm sure it was, but you gave a

fantastic speech in the church. You really are a strong woman."

"Caleb I wanted to thank you for coming to the church today, you didn't need to do that. Also, thanks for helping Kammie and Luca with the house, it was perfect, thanks."

"No problem Tasha I told you I would be there for you, I don't renege, remember."

"Thanks Caleb you really are wonderful." did I just say that out loud, I can feel myself blushing.

"Thanks that means a lot to me, I'm sure you're exhausted and need to rest so I will talk to you soon ok." I feel like he is trying to get me off the phone quickly, maybe he was busy and I interrupted him.

"I am tired Caleb, I'm sorry if I disturbed you I just wanted to thank you. Good night."

"Good night my Angel, hope you sleep well tonight." and he hangs up.

I turn my phone off and lay back in the bed, I think of Felix and the good times and I start to fall asleep, Caleb's face is the one I see before I drift away.

4

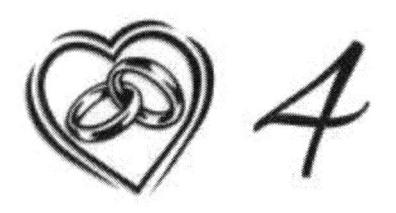

I wake up sweating, and I'm in the corner of my room just rocking back and forth, Mum is in front of me on her knees. "Tasha it's ok it's over now, come on wake up." she reaches out to touch me and I flinch. She looks sad.

"I'm not going to hurt you baby girl." she reaches out again and this time I let her take me into her arms.

I lean into her and cry, "I thought I would be able to sleep now that he's gone."

"I know but today was the funeral Tasha, it was a very emotional day. I know you were trying to only think of the good times but your subconscious can only remember the bad times. Come on let's go downstairs, Dad went down to make cocoa."

she smiles at me and I feel like I'm a child again.

She helps me up off the floor, takes my hand and we walk down to the kitchen. Dad is there when we go in and he smiles at me "I thought you might like some cocoa."

"Thanks Dad I'd love some." Dad puts the cups of cocoa down on the kitchen table and we all sit down.

Nobody says anything for about 5 minutes and then Mum asks, "Do you want to tell us about your dream Tasha?"

I take a deep sigh, a sip of cocoa and tell them, "I was dreaming about Felix and all the good times we had together, it was a really nice dream. Then I dreamt about the funeral and Felix wasn't really dead, he was waiting for us back at the house. When everyone had left I was on my own and he started calling my name, I looked everywhere and I found him in the bedroom, he was naked and waiting for me. He told me that he never loved me, that he had used me as a means to having sex on tap. He said that he wanted to work in Clifton Associates and when I was looking for a job he spoke to them and encouraged them to employ me. He told me that I wasn't worth the hassle that I had given him in the last few months and he had faked his death so that he could kill me. Mum it felt so real, he was horrible to me. I woke up when he started hitting me, my body hurts even though I know it was a dream."

"Tasha you have been through so much in the last 6 months and your mind is having a hard time processing everything. I'm sure you will continue to have nightmares, but as long as you are here with us, we will look after you. We love you unconditionally Tasha." Mum says hugging me to her.

"I find it really hard to think about what Felix did to you, I wanted to kill him myself when I found out, but you wanted to give him a chance to get better, you thought he would get better. It broke my heart to think of him hurting you over and over again and you not telling anyone." Dad says and I know he is holding back the tears.

"I told Caleb some of it Dad, he was there and I knew I could talk to him if I wanted to talk to someone."

"I know that now Tasha, but as a parent it hurts when your own child feels they can't talk to you about something so important." He looks down at the table.

"Dad, I'm sorry," I'm sobbing now, my heart is breaking that I made him feel like this. "I … I… I didn't think you would believe me, Felix was always perfect in yours and Mum's eyes. I thought you'd think I was attention seeking or something."

"Tasha don't you think we would have listened to you? We love you and we would have taken your word over anything. You have never been an attention seeker, why wouldn't we have believed you? Tasha you are everything to us and even if we thought you were attention seeking then we still would have looked into something that serious." Dad takes my hand and holds it between his two big hands.

I look up and all I can see is unconditional love in his eyes, "I'm sorry Dad, I should have trusted both of you to believe me, it's just that when it was all happening I didn't really want to believe it myself that it was happening. Does that make sense?"

"Of course it makes sense baby girl, I'm not giving out to you, I just want you to know that we are here for you whenever you need us. We love you Tasha and you have been so brave, we are so proud of you," Dad kisses my hand and then says, "now come on its 4.30 in the morning, we need to go to sleep, will you be ok baby girl?"

"Yes, I'll be fine Dad, thank you so much, I know I'm loved and I need to focus on that and not how much hatred there was in my life recently." We all stand and put our cups into the sink and then we go up to bed, when we reach the top of the stairs, Dad takes me into a hug and tells me he loves me, so does Mum. I then climb into bed and have a really good night's sleep.

5

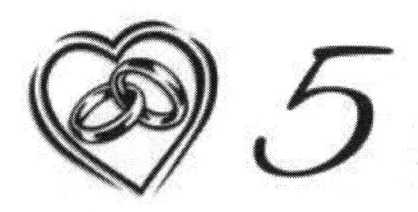

When I wake up in the morning, I go down for breakfast and then try to decide what to do with my day. Me, Mum and Dad talk about my house and whether I should put it on the market as I'm not sure I want to live in it with the memories that I have. Unfortunately, my memories are tainted by the last month or so and I can't seem to get any of the good memories back. We ring around estate agents to see what kind of price I can get for the house and then we arrange a few viewings. The house is still tidy from when Kammie, Luca and Caleb cleaned it up and it is the perfect time for the estate agent to come and see it and take pictures. I know the market is slow right now, but I'm not in a hurry to sell it.

We go for lunch at The White Lion Bar and just have a relaxing, quiet day. It seems to be a day for reflecting on what happened and how I can move on. When we have finished lunch and are sitting drinking coffee Mum says, "Tasha, me and Dad have been talking and we think you should go and see the counsellor, what was her name? Sally, that's it!"

"I know you're right Mum, I was hoping I could cope with this on my own and didn't need any other help, but I suppose it won't hurt to ring her and make an appointment." I smile and I see Mum physically relax, she obviously thought she was going to have a fight on her hands.

"That's great Tasha, I'm delighted, we will take you in and wait for you, you don't have to do this on your own, we are here to help you always." she says smiling.

"Thanks Mum, I know you both are here for me."

Dad drops me and Mum into the city so that we can look around the shops and so that I can get myself some new clothes for work and I want to have my hair cut, I suppose I want to treat myself and feel like Tasha again.

We walk around chatting and laughing, I feel a little bit guilty about having fun when Felix is only just buried, but he made me think that I was worthless over the last couple of months and I need this for me.

On the way to lunch I show Mum where the office to Blue Eye is, it's a magnificent building and we walk past and look into reception. I can't believe I will be starting work there on Monday. The girl on reception looks up and smiles at me, she gives me a little wave and then she has to answer the phone. "Wow, that was nice of her Tasha, she obviously recognised you. I think you will be very happy working there, I didn't think it was the right thing for you to do, to go back to work so quick after the funeral, but knowing you as much as I do then I think it is the right thing. I hope Caleb agrees and lets you start work early, but if I know him at all, he will agree with whatever you want." she smiles as she says this last part.

"Thanks Mum, I think so too, it will take my mind off these horrible things and at least I can concentrate on something different instead of thinking about Felix all the time."

We cross the road and go into TGI's where we order some platters and a cocktail each, me and Mum haven't done this for a few years and I used to always enjoy it.

I text Caleb to tell him that I am in the City and to let him know that I am feeling good today, I don't tell him about my nightmare though.

"Hey Caleb, me and Mum are in town and I just showed her the building where I'm going to start working ☺"

"Really, you should have said I would have brought you both in for the guided tour ☺!"

"Ha ha, I'm sure you would have, but I know you are busy. You probably have lots to do for your new member of staff lol"

"Not really, I just have to get ready for not being able to hold your hand or sit down and chat, but I'll manage"

"Of course we can sit down and chat Caleb, why wouldn't we be able to do that?"

"Tasha I won't be able to sit and chat because everyone would know how I feel about you and you're not ready for that, yet"

What does he mean by that? I'm not even going to think about what he could possibly mean.

"Caleb, we are both professional we will be able to chat without anyone knowing we are friends, I promise I won't jump on you lol"

I can't believe I said that – where did it come from?

"Damn I was hoping you would ☺. Tasha I have to go there is another call waiting for me, I hate to rush you off the line, we don't get to talk often enough for me to rush you."

"That's ok my lunch has arrived anyway, I'll talk to you later ok"

"I look forward to it Angel"

I love it when he calls me "Angel", it makes my insides tighten and I catch my breath.

Me and Mum end up staying in TGI's for a couple of hours and we had a few too many cocktails, we have talked, we have laughed and we have cried. Dad has had to come in to collect us and he doesn't look too happy that we are a bit drunk. "God, I leave you two women alone for a couple of hours and look at the state of you." he says, maneuvering the car back into the busy streets.

Oh dear, I haven't seen Dad angry since the other day when he went outside and cried. I look at him in the rear view mirror and say, "Dad are you really mad with us, we both needed to just let loose."

He starts laughing, "of course I'm not mad, I would have joined you if I knew you were going to have a few drinks."

Thank god he's not mad. "Dad you got

me there, I really thought you were mad." I start laughing and so does Mum.

When we get home I lay on the couch and just chill out, it was a fun day but I'm so tired. I must have fallen asleep because I get woken by my phone signaling a text, I smile hoping it's Caleb.

"Hey Angel, how was the rest of your afternoon?"

"It was fun, we stayed for a couple of hours and had quite a few cocktails. How was yours?"

"It wasn't as much fun as yours, some of us had work to do lol. I found it hard to picture you just over the road and not to go over and sit with you for a while."

"You could have done that if you wanted, I'm not sure what Mum would have thought but she would have been ok"

"Maybe another time, I just wanted to sit with you really, just to make sure you are ok and to see if you needed to talk"

"Thank you Caleb, you really are very thoughtful and I don't think I tell you often enough, but I'm so glad to have you in my life, you make each day easier than the last"

What is wrong with me? It must be the drink, I'm not normally this forward.

"Angel that makes me so happy, I want you to be happy, I don't like seeing you sad. I have a feeling that your life going forward will be a good life and I hope that I am in your future. Actually no, I want to be your future"

I don't know what to say to that, how can I reply? He means so much to me and I know that our relationship will develop, I can feel it developing already. Can I really do this to Felix? So soon after he killed himself? I'm having doubts now, I should be in mourning for my husband but I can't bring myself to mourn him. The Felix I knew and married died a couple of months ago in my mind, the Felix that hung himself was not my Felix. I know it sounds harsh, but what he did to me will scar me for life and I can't forgive him yet, I just can't. I want to see Caleb for what he is – he is a loving, compassionate man who wants me! He sees me for who I am and not what he wants me to be, does that make sense?

"I don't know what my future holds yet Caleb, but I want you in my life, you have been there for me and helped me through shit that I would never have expected to have to deal with. You have been a constant in my life for the last couple of months and for that I thank you. You mean everything to me and I want you in my future."

"Angel, words fail me."

"Oh ok, is that good? ☺"

"Of course it's good Tasha, it's not very often I'm speechless, you better not tell anyone lol"

"Ha ha, I'll just enjoy it while I can then"

"Not for long My Angel, not for long. I wish I could meet you for coffee, I want to hug you and look after you."

"Well let's meet for coffee then, I'd like to see you to say thank you for helping with the house and I have something I want to ask you"

"Sounds intriguing, yeah I can meet for coffee, I can't do tomorrow Tasha, I have back to back meetings until 6pm."

"No of course you're busy, I understand, it's fine honestly don't worry about it"

"Of course I'll meet you, I can meet you for dinner tonight if you want or coffee another day"

"Can you do Saturday? You might have something planned though, it's ok"

"Saturday is fine, will we say about 11am?"

"Yeah that's perfect, will I meet you in the same place as last time?"

"No, I'll come collect you from your parent's house if that's ok"

"Erm yeah that's fine, I look forward to it, it will be good to see you again Caleb"

"Yeah I missed you too, see you tomorrow Tasha"

I didn't say I missed him, he obviously thought because I said it would be good to see him again that I missed him. Well I suppose if I think about it I did. I've only just buried my husband I shouldn't be thinking about Caleb in that way, but I can't help it, he has helped me through the hardest part of my relationship, he is always there for me day or night.

I wonder whether he will notice my new hair style or not, I hope he does.

We don't have dinner because we were out at lunch and me and Mum had a platter along with the cocktails, so we just sit in the lounge watching TV and talking. I love being here with my parents, I know the time will come when I want to do my own thing, but for now this is where I want to be.

Before we go to bed, Dad makes some cocoa. "I'm hoping that if we have it now we won't need to wake up in the middle of the night to have it." he smiles and I know he is joking and hoping that I don't have any nightmares tonight.

"Thanks Dad, I'm sure I won't be waking up in the middle of the night now." I smile at him and we all drink out cocoa.

    I'm exhausted when I get to the top of the stairs and I drag myself into bed and fall asleep really quickly.

6

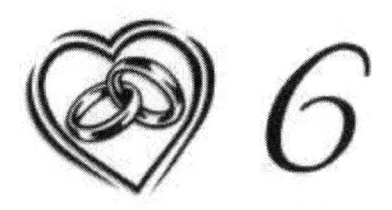

When I wake up I see the sun streaming through my window, not only did I have a nightmare free night, I slept in too. I feel like today is going to be a good day. I wish I was seeing Caleb today, but it won't be long to wait until tomorrow. I send him a quick text before I get out of bed, because I know he will be in meetings all day.

"Morning Caleb, I've just woken up and it's such a beautiful day. I know you are going to be busy today and I don't expect to hear from you, so I thought I'd tell you that I was thinking about you. Hope today isn't too busy and you get chance to relax a bit ☺"

I don't get a reply; he must have gone into his first meeting already. I get up and go into the bathroom to have a shower, I feel more positive today than I have for a while. I scrub myself clean and feel like I am scrubbing away Felix and with every drop of water that goes down the drain so do all my bad memories, or at least I hope they do.

After I have dried my hair and got dressed I go downstairs, Mum and Dad aren't there which is strange as they are always here in the mornings. I ring Mum's mobile, "Hey mum where are you? It was weird coming down and the house empty."

"Hi we are out food shopping, we won't be long." she says and I can hear the hustle and bustle of the supermarket.

"Ok it's not a problem, I just wondered that's all." I say and she says she will be home soon. I hang up and then kick myself, I don't need to know where they are every minute of the day, they don't ask that of me so I shouldn't ask them either. This living at home thing is starting to become difficult.

I do my laundry today and realise that I actually don't have a lot of my stuff here with me, I don't want to go to the house until I really need to. I'll just have to make do, as long as I stay on top of the laundry then I'll be fine.

At lunchtime I tell Mum and Dad that I will be seeing Caleb the next day to thank him for helping with the house, Mum says that it was very good of him to help out and that he is a wonderful man. I smile because she is so right. She knows that I am going to ask him if I can start work a week early, we had this discussion yesterday. Now, she thinks it might be the best thing for me to do, she reminds me though that something might happen to trigger my grieving process and that her and dad will be there to help pick up the pieces.

"Mum, I'm fine, after what Felix did to me I forgave him but told him I wasn't going back to him, I know I should still be grieving for him, but I can't get past the memories he left me with. He deliberately lured me to the house so that I would be the one who found him hanging, how do you think that makes me feel?" I know I am starting to shout and get upset and I promised myself that I wouldn't. "How could he hate me so much that he would subject me to that kind of pain?"

"Tasha, I don't know how I would feel in the same situation, I don't know why he wanted you to find him like that, I don't know why he did those things to you and you are the only one who knows when and how to grieve for your loss, but I still think you need to really think about how you feel and take the time to grieve your loss. Me and your Dad are here for you when that happens and we know it could be at any time now or in the future." She comes over and hugs me.

I tell them that I have an appointment with the counsellor, Sally this afternoon and Dad offers to take me. I'm not looking forward to it, but after the last time I felt much better, hopefully this will help me too.

He drops me off and tells me that he will wait for me in the usual place, The Cozy Place Coffee Shop. I said I would meet him there after I have finished.

I find myself sitting in the waiting room and thinking about Felix, I know that she will ask me how I feel so I think about it and I really can't answer that question. I don't know how I feel or how I should feel.

I'm in a world of my own when I hear a voice, "Natasha, come on in." I stand and follow her to her office.

"Hi Sally, thank you for seeing me at such short notice." I had only rung this morning, I was surprised when she said she had a slot available.

"It's fine, I read about Felix in the newspaper and thought you might be in to see me soon." She sits down and shuffles some of her papers on her desk. "So tell me what happened since the last time I saw you."

I sit and tell her about how I had told Felix in the hospital that I wasn't moving back in with him and how he had reacted to that news. I then told her that he'd text me on Sunday to ask me to come and collect some of my stuff and that he had seemed to accept what was happening between us. I stop and think for a while and then tell her how I found him and what happened when Dad and Luca turned up.

"That must have been terrible for you Natasha, why do you think he did that? Why did he ring you and get you to come around on your own knowing you would find him?"

"I don't know Sally, I just don't know. I think it is one of the worst things that he did to me, the rapes, assaults and punches were nothing in comparison to what he did to me that day." I break down crying, I knew this would happen, but I need to talk to someone who will just listen.

"It seems like Felix wanted to hurt you one final time. It was very cruel what he did to you, how do you feel now that he is dead?"

Wow, she is blunt if nothing else. "I feel like a weight has been lifted off my shoulders and that I don't have to think about what Felix will think if I do this or that. Then on the other side I feel guilty that he has only just been buried and here I am getting on with my life. I am hoping that I can start my new job next week instead of the week after, because I am sick of sitting at home waiting for this injury to heal or for that bruise to not show anymore. Then I feel bad because his Mum and Dad won't see him again and I still get to live the rest of my life." I'm not crying but I am feeling emotional, it's very difficult to feel both of those emotions at the same time and it is very confusing.

"Natasha, those are the emotions I would expect you to feel because what happened to you was very drastic and I think you forget everything that went on in the house, take away the big beatings, rapes, assaults and think about the small things. Like picking your clothes for you – that is extremely controlling and for you not to have that is liberating to you. He called you names – that makes you lose confidence in yourself and it will take a while for you to be totally confident again, but I can see it starting to happen already. To be honest I thought you would be a total mess coming in here today, no offence, but I am surprised that you are very well put together. You must have wonderful family and friends who have helped you through this difficult time."

"Yes I do, they have all been amazing and I can feel myself getting more confident every day. However, I don't know how I will feel when the time comes for me to have a relationship again, but I realise that I have to deal with that at the time it happens and not to worry about it before it does."

"Absolutely Natasha, wow you inspire

me, you are such a strong woman and never let another person tell you any different. I'm here whenever you need to talk to me, just give me a ring."

I guess that's it then it's over. It wasn't as hard as I expected it to be and I actually feel lighter for having talked to a professional person about it. We both stand up and she walks me to the door, I hold out my hand to shake hers and she surprises me by leaning forward and hugging me. "You truly are amazing Natasha, take care."

"Thank you for everything you have done for me Sally I really appreciate it." I turn and leave and I go to meet Dad in the coffee shop. He smiles when I walk in.

"I guess that went well then," he says, I look at him questioning his comment, "you look like a different person Tasha, you don't look like you have the world on your shoulders anymore, I'm so glad you went to see her."

I hug him and then we drive home to Mum and tell her what happened with Sally.

7

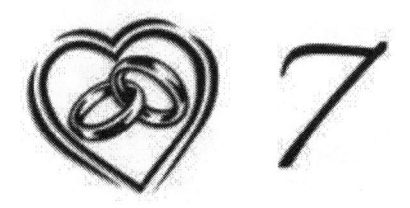

Saturday comes and it's time for Caleb to collect me, I've put on some of my new clothes and my new hairstyle still looks good. He comes up and knocks on the door, I open the door and invite him in, I'm quite nervous seeing him again and knowing that I will be alone in his company. He smiles from ear to ear and comes inside, "Good morning Jean" he says to my Mum "How are you?" he holds out his hand for her to shake.

"Morning Caleb, I'm good thank you." she says shaking his hand. "Thank you for helping Kammie and Luca with the house, it was very kind of you."

"It was no problem, I didn't want Tasha to have to do it, that's why I offered." he turns to me, "Are you ready to go?"

I nod my head, say goodbye to Mum and Dad and then we turn and walk out of the door. He opens the door to the car for me to slip inside, he closes the door and then walks round to his side. Once he gets in he fastens his seatbelt and then we are off. He drives for about 20 minutes and I notice we are driving out into the countryside. "Where are we going Caleb?" I ask looking around me.

"We are going to my house on the beach." he says smiling at me.

"House on the beach? OK! How many houses do you have?" I laugh but I'm actually nervous, I haven't really thought about him being the CEO, to me he's just Caleb, an ordinary guy.

He laughs back at me, "I only have this house and my apartment in the City Centre. I tend to stay in the apartment during the week so that I'm close for work and then come out here at the weekends."

"OK." I say because I don't know what else to say. I sit there in silence for a while and then I can see the sea and the beach. "Oh Caleb it's beautiful, I can see why you like to come out here to get away from everything." I say looking out to sea.

"I know I love it here, this is my sanctuary." he says and I can feel the contentment coming off him. He pulls into a driveway and the house is literally on the beach, it is amazing. He turns the engine off, then he is out of the car and walking around to my side of the car where he opens the door and holds his hand out for me to take to get out of the car. I take his hand and I feel something between us, I look at him and he smiles at me, he felt it too.

I don't let go of his hand as he guides me into the house. Inside is as beautiful as the outside, and he takes me straight through to the decking area he has leading onto the beach. We stand side by side leaning against the railing just looking out to sea. "Caleb, how can you leave this house and stay in the City? I think I could stay here forever and just look out at this all the time." I'm still looking out to sea, it is so tranquil and I feel at peace. The sea looks a real sparkling blue colour, like diamonds glinting in the sun. When I look to my left or my right all I can see is beach, it's a sandy beach – the best in my opinion – it's very clean and there are dunes in the background. There is a cliff off to the right and I can just about see small people on the top of the cliff looking down at the sea. It's so beautiful!

"I used to live here all the time and travel in and out of the City, but it became too much and I had to get my apartment. That's why I always enjoy coming back here and staying for a couple of days. It's my escape Tasha, my bolt hole." he says and turns to me, "I don't bring anyone here, this is my place and my place alone."

"Really, then why have you brought me here Caleb?" I turn to him, why has he brought me here?

"You're not just anyone, you are someone special and I thought you needed a sanctuary Tasha, somewhere you can relax and enjoy the surroundings." he holds his hand out and takes mine, I let him. We stand for another few minutes looking out across the beach and then he turns and says, "Come on let me show you the rest of the house and then I'll make lunch." he pulls me back into the house.

I laugh because he seems to be so excited to show me his house. He shows me the kitchen, which is huge and the window looks out onto the beach and also the lounge which has a picture window and a huge open fire in the middle of the room, it looks like a fire pit, I bet it's fabulous when it's lit.

When he's finished showing me downstairs, he leads me up the stairs to the spare room, which is an extremely large double room with an en suite, this room looks out at the back of the house so the view isn't as good. He shows me the master bathroom, which has a large Jacuzzi bath in it, I bet that is sumptuous to sink into. Then he takes me through to the master bedroom, wow, this room is unbelievable, the master bed is huge and there are walk in wardrobes with sliding doors which are hidden in the wall. Walking through the picture window onto the veranda we are back looking at the beach again. "Caleb this place is fantastic, thank you so much for bringing me here." I turn to face him and I smile at him.

"I'm so glad you like it Tasha, I don't like bringing people here because it is my escape from the corporate world and I like to keep it to myself. I was worried about bringing you here because I wanted you to like it, it means so much to me that you do." He is so thoughtful and he wears his heart on his sleeve, that is so alien to me. He turns to face me and he pulls me into a hug, I can feel my heart start to speed up, he puts his finger under my chin and tips my head up so that I am looking up at him. "It means a lot to me that you like it here and that you are happy when you are here. I can see in your eyes that you do like it and that makes me very happy." he rests his chin on the top of my head and just holds me tight.

I don't say anything because I don't need to. After about 5 minutes he pulls away and then takes my hand and pulls me back through the bedroom and down the stairs. When we were walking out of his bedroom, I couldn't help but think about him sleeping in the bed, all ruffled and his hair all muzzy. I shake my head to get rid of those thoughts from my mind.

He pulls me into the kitchen and pulls out a seat at the breakfast bar, "Sit Tasha, sit and talk to me while I cook." he smiles at me.

I hop up onto the seat and lean against the breakfast bar and watch him as he works. "You can cook? That surprises me Caleb. How did you learn?"

Caleb is a super chef, lunch is amazing and he's great company. He tells me about how he learned to cook from his Mum, he used to sit in the kitchen when she was cooking and then he kept asking questions about what she did so she showed him how to cook. He tells me how he started his company when he was fresh out of university and then how he grew it to the company it is today. He sounds so proud it makes my heart soar. We talk about his family who live in Weston Super Mare, he obviously loves them a lot. I ask him about starting work a week early and he thinks it is a great idea, he knows that I need something to occupy my mind, to help me past these last few weeks.

Before I know it, it is 4pm, we've been talking for hours. "Do you want to go for a walk on the beach before I take you back?" He asks.

"I'd love that Caleb." I reach out and take the hand he offered to me. I smile at him and we walk down the stairs leading from the decking. We walk in silence looking around, it's beautiful and so peaceful. All of a sudden I get a burst of energy, I look around me, "First one to reach the jetty over there doesn't pay for the next coffee we have." I smile at him.

He smiles back, "Ok but you'll need a head start."

"What?!?" I laugh.

"3, 2, 1 GO!" He shouts.

I start running like my life depends on it because I know he will pass me out but I need to look like I am making an effort because what I really want is to lose.

After he finishes counting to 30 he starts running after me, god he can run fast, he's catching up with me. I'm looking at him rather than where I'm going and I trip over some seaweed on the sand, I can feel myself going in slow motion face first. I land with a humph and start laughing so loud. Next thing I know Caleb is beside me and he is rolling me over, I have tears coming down my face because it is so funny, only I could be so clumsy.

"Tasha are you ok? You're crying, where does it hurt?" he says as his hands start rubbing all over my body to see where it hurts. I stop laughing because all I can concentrate on is his hands, he slows down and looks at me, "Did you do that on purpose so I would have to touch you all over, my Angel?" He asks smiling down at me.

"No honest I fell." I laugh because it

seems so silly. Before I know it his hands are wiping my tears, brushing my hair back of my face and then his lips are on mine, slowly at first but when I run my fingers through his hair and pull him close everything becomes more urgent. I feel myself getting lost in all that is Caleb, his lips are so soft, his tongue is piercing and his groans are such a turn on.

After what seems like an hour he starts to pull away slowly and then he looks down at me. He looks at my lips and then he looks up into my eyes, "Tasha I don't want to apologise for that because it really was beautiful, but I don't want you to run from me or feel guilty for that. There is a connection between us that I have never felt before and I don't think I ever will again. It's like you were sent to me so that I can look after you." he pushes my hair back off my face and then leans down slowly and kisses my lips softly and gently, then he sits up and pulls me to a sitting position. I know he is waiting for me to say something but I really don't know what to say. It was the most amazing kiss I've ever had in my life and I'm confused and frightened. I gave my heart and soul to Felix and look at what he did to me, I don't think I can do it again!

"Caleb you don't need to apologise, I feel a connection to you too and that frightens me. I've had my heart totally squashed recently as you know and I don't know if I can give it away again, at least not straight away." Why does it feel like my heart is breaking, I don't want to hurt him and I don't want to lose him as a friend either. "Oh and by the way, it was amazing for me too." I smile at him because it really was.

"Yeah it was, I would never do anything to hurt you or break your heart Tasha and I hope you know that. I will wait for you to be ready because you're worth it to me." He leans forward and kisses me very gently on the lips again. "Now come on lets go back to the house, I think you won the race because you were the closest so coffee is on me next time." he starts laughing.

"No way that's not fair, you would have won if I hadn't been clumsy and fallen over. Anyway it's my turn for coffee." I punch him in the arm and laugh.

"Ow," he says laughing and rubbing his arm, "now who's playing dirty and rough."

"I'm sorry," I say in between laughing, "but I think I hurt my hand more than your arm hurts." I rub my hand up and down his arm, wow his muscles are so hard, I realise what I am doing and take my hand away. I look up into his eyes and he reaches out and takes my hand that I punched him with and brings it up to his lips and kisses it very gently.

"I would say that serves you right, but I don't want you to hurt, you are so delicate."

he takes my hand and we walk back to the house in silence, nothing needs to be said.

When we get to the house, we go inside and he makes me a coffee, "I will be paying for the next one, but this one is to warm you up after our walk on the beach."

"Thanks Caleb, I've had a good day, and it's taken my mind off things at home." I lean up and kiss him on the cheek, "I don't deserve you in my life, you are far too good for me." he starts to say something and I reach up and put my finger to his lips to shush him, "but I think I would find it very difficult not to have you in my life now, you've come into my world and it's like you have always been there, I feel like I can talk to you about anything. Thank you Caleb for always being there for me." I smile at him and lean in closer and put my arms around him and hug him to me.

"Wow Tasha that means so much to me." he says putting his arms around me, "I feel like my life only just started when I met you, nothing that happened before means anything to me, all I want is for you to be happy and that will make me happy. As I said earlier I have never felt like this about anyone before and it does feel strange but at the same time, it feels like this is what I am meant to do." he rests his chin on the top of my head. "Now come on I'm going to take you home before your Mum and Dad come and find you." he pulls away and I suddenly feel cold.

I gather my things and we walk out to his car, he opens the door for me and then walks to his side of the car and gets in. He turns on the engine and drives back to Bristol and back to my parent's house. He is quiet in the car and I know he is thinking about something he wants to talk about.

"Caleb what is it? I know you want to say something." I say reaching out and placing my hand on top of his on the gear stick. He turns his head to look at me and smiles.

"You're so intuitive Tasha, I was thinking about work on Monday and how hard it will be to see you so close and not be able to touch you or just sit and talk to you like today." he looks out the window.

"Are you sorry that I took the job? Do you want me to refuse the job? If you do then I would do that for you." I say not able to look at him because I can feel the tears forming in my eyes.

All of a sudden the car pulls off the road, he jumps out of the car and runs around to my side and opens my door, he squats down and takes my hands, "Tasha that's not what I meant at all, but you would do that for me?" he seems surprised.

"Yes I would Caleb, if you would find it difficult to work with me then yes I wouldn't start and I would look for another job."

He rubs my hands and just sits there looking at them for a few minutes then he pulls them up to his face and he puts them on his cheek and he leans into my hands, "Tasha, I'm just sorry that I won't be able to do this on Monday and hold your hand, or have coffee in the canteen without people talking. I want to make your transition into the company as smooth as possible for you, you've been through a lot this last while and I don't want to make it any harder for you. Do you understand that?" he says as he still nuzzles into my hand.

"Yes I do and thank you so much for always thinking of me. We will be fine, you're my friend and I am so grateful to have you in my life Caleb." I turn my hand so that it is cupping his cheek and then I pull him closer to me, I can't help myself I need to feel his lips on mine again, so I pull him to my lips and I kiss him with as much passion as I can muster. I hear him groan and I pull away, "Caleb I feel like I need you in my life to make me happy, to keep me alive and that won't change because I work for you, so don't think about it too much, it will work out the way it will work out." He looks at me in shock and then smiles at me.

"Ok Tasha, we can do this." he stands and walks back to his side of the car and then drives off.

When we get back to my house I ask whether he wants to come in but he declines, "Maybe another time, I think your Mum and Dad will be asking enough questions without me coming in too."

He smiles at me and then he walks back down the path to his car and rolls down the window and shouts, "See you on Monday my new employee," and then he is gone from sight.

8

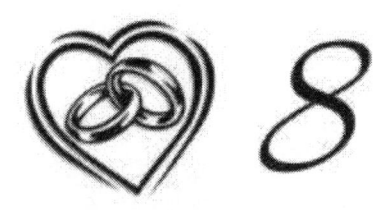

When I go in the house, Mum and Dad are not there waiting for me which is surprising, so I go and lie down on my bed and think about today, about Caleb, about Felix and about my new job. I feel like I am betraying Felix by even thinking about Caleb, but I shake that notion off because of how he was to me at the end. My phone rings and its Kammie, "Hi bitch," she says, "what are you up to?"

"Hey Kammie, I'm just laying on my bed thinking about things and my new job that I'm starting on Monday."

"Really you're going back to work so soon, maybe it's what you need, I know you don't like sitting around and want to get on with your life. So, with that in mind do you want to go out tonight, just for some food and a few drinks?" she sounds apprehensive because she thinks I'll say no it's too soon.

"Yeah why not Kammie, I haven't been out since that night in Jesters, yeah let's do it." I say smiling.

We make our plans to meet at TGI's and then see where the night takes us. When we hang up I look into my wardrobe and realise that I need to go and collect some clothes from my house. I jump in my car and drive to my house. It feels strange coming back here, but I walk into the house and straight up to my bedroom. I take out some clothes that I will use for work and then what I need for tonight.

While I'm sitting on the bed thinking about Felix there is a knock at the front door. Who is it? I go down the stairs carefully and open the door, it's the Estate Agent, I forgot I had rung them and told them I was going to the house if they wanted to come and take photos.

I wander around the house with the photographer as they compliment the house and take photos. Once they have finished I say goodbye and then take a last look around the house, lock the door and drive back to Mum's.

When I get there Mum and Dad have come back and they wondered where, I was especially when my car was missing.

"I went to the house to let the photographer in and to pick up some clothes for work next week and Kammie has asked me to go out tonight for dinner, I said yes if that's ok?"

"Of course it is Tasha, you are old enough and lived away from home for such a long time you don't have to ask us if you can go out." Mum starts laughing.

I laugh as well because the thought of me asking is actually funny. As Mum makes dinner for her and Dad we talk about Caleb's house on the beach, I tell her how wonderful it is and how much she would love it. I don't tell her about the kiss, some things should be kept secret.

After dinner I go upstairs and get ready for meeting Kammie, I'm assuming Luca is coming with us but text her to say I don't mind if he does.

"Hey, I assume Luca is coming with us tonight? It's fine with me if he does honestly, he's like a best friend to me anyway"

"Thanks Tasha I thought you would say that but I didn't want to assume either"

"No worries, see you at 8.30pm"

"☺"

    I put on a sapphire blue dress I haven't worn before because Felix always said it made me look tarty, but I don't think it does. Its figure hugging and low at the neckline and at the back, it compliments my red hair superbly. I style my hair so that it is swept to one side at the back and then it hangs down on one side. When I go downstairs, Dad whistles at me. I laugh, "Wow Tasha, I haven't seen you looking like that for a few years, I can see now how much Felix smothered you and took your personality away from you, he made the decisions for you without you even realising."

    "I think you're right Dad, every time I took this dress out he told me I was too old to wear anything like this, I just didn't realise what he was doing at the time." I smile at Dad and then go over and hug him, "I love you Dad."

    He smiles back at me, "I know." We both laugh, he always says this because he doesn't like getting soppy.

    We get in the car, he is driving me into town so that I only need to get a taxi home. I get out of the car and walk into the restaurant and I see that Kammie and Luca are already there waiting for me, they are deep in conversation and I can see he is holding her hand. I hope they make a go of it because they are well suited.

"Hey guys, can anyone join in or is this a private party?" I say pulling the chair out and sitting down.

"Hey bitch," Kammie says and she lets go of Luca's hand.

"You don't need to do that you know Kammie, I don't mind you getting together, I actually think you make a great couple." I smile at her.

She laughs, "Thank god for that I was worried about telling you."

After that we just talked and laughed, it was great to laugh so much. I told them about my day with Caleb, obviously leaving out the bit about the kiss, that's for my memories only.

We eat dinner and then we start talking about whether we want to go clubbing or not, I don't mind either way.

"Can we go to Jesters Tasha? Are you alright with that?" Luca asks me.

"Why would that bother me?" I ask him confused.

"Because of what happened the last time you were there." he says unable to meet my eyes.

"Luca, Kammie, seriously it's ok, I'm not going to break down at the mention of anything to do with Felix, I've accepted what he did to me, I've forgiven him and now I just want to move on. Let's just think about it as a new beginning, now let's go and party." I say looking from one to the other.

"Ok Tasha, I'm sorry but I care about you and I don't want you to be uncomfortable." he says.

"Right come on then, lets pay the bill and then we can go and party." I say linking their arms in between them.

9

We pay the bill and then we walk over to Jesters and join the queue that is already forming. After about 5 minutes a bouncer comes down the line and says, "Miss, are you Natasha?"

"Yes I am why?" I'm confused how does he know me?

"You don't need to queue you can come straight in and your friends too." I turn and look at Luca and Kammie to see if they are confused, they don't seem as confused as me. "What's going on guys?" I ask them.

They both shake their heads as if to say they don't know so I go up to the bouncer and link his arm, "Why don't I have to queue?"

"The boss said that you should skip the queue." he says.

"Well, you tell your boss thank you I was getting cold." I laugh because in all the years I have stood in a queue for a nightclub I have never been able to skip.

We go inside and then when we try to pay they won't let us, "The boss says you're not to pay." Ok now I'm curious who this boss is. I turn to look at Luca and say, "Luca, do I know the boss of this club or do you? I'm confused here."

"Don't ask me I don't know anything." he says shaking his head.

We go into the nightclub and up to the bar and order a round of Sambuca's with our drinks, I intend to drink and forget everything tonight.

We have been in the nightclub drinking Sambuca chasers for about half an hour and then I decide that I want to dance, so I drag Kammie out to the dance floor and start shaking my bootie.

We must have been on the dance floor for nearly an hour when Kammie says that she needs to go back to Luca, so she goes off and I stay dancing. All of a sudden I can feel that there is someone behind me and I can feel them getting closer, I start to feel panicky because this person is dancing very close to me, copying my moves. All of a sudden I feel a hand come around my stomach, but instead of feeling scared it makes me feel safe. The only person who can make me feel safe is Caleb, so I move back until my body is touching his and I start to move slowly and I can feel him moving along with me. He leans down and kisses my neck on the side where I don't have my hair, "Hello my Angel how did you know it was me? Or do you dance like this with everyone?" he chuckles and I know it's not jealousy or possessiveness which drives this question.

"I felt safe and then I knew it was you Caleb." I move back until there is no room between us and I can feel every muscle in his body against mine.

"You look beautiful tonight Tasha, I couldn't watch you any longer without coming over to you," he whispers into my ear and I can feel his breath tickling my ear, suddenly he kisses just under my ear very gently, "I'm so glad you came here tonight Tasha, I haven't stopped thinking about you since this afternoon, I hope I didn't frighten you away." he kisses me again heading towards my collar bone.

I've stopped dancing now and am just resting against his body, "I've been thinking about you too Caleb and no you didn't frighten me away, you couldn't do that, you make me feel too safe and wanted."

"Oh you're wanted alright." he says as his other hand comes around to my stomach and takes my hand and then all of a sudden he spins me around so that I am facing him but my body is still so close to his body. I look up at him and I know that I want to kiss him, but something in my mind is telling me it's not the right thing to do, here and now.

"Tasha there you are," its Kammie, "come on lets go to the bar, are you coming with us Caleb?" she says not missing a beat. We walk off the dance floor and towards the bar where I see Kammie and Luca. We sit at the table with them and they don't make Caleb feel unwelcome.

He asks what everyone wants and goes to the bar, I go with him to help him carry the drinks. After he orders the drinks he talks to the barmaid and laughs with her. He then introduces me, "Claire, this is Tasha a dear friend."

I smile at her and say, "Nice to meet you Claire." she says the same back. I'm not really sure why he is introducing me to her, but he obviously knows her well.

He takes the drinks and walks off without paying, I take the rest of the drinks and just smile at Claire, maybe he has a tab or something. He obviously comes here often, I'll have to ask him.

We give out the drinks and then we sit. I take a sip of my drink and then say, "So Caleb, do you come here often?" I start laughing at the stupid comment and they all join in with me thank god.

"Yes, I do actually Tasha, a few times a week." he says smiling. Who the hell goes clubbing three times a week at our age. I look at him strangely maybe there's something I don't know about him. Maybe he comes to pick up random girls and maybe I was more of a challenge to him than he expected and he has been nice to me to achieve his original goal. I can feel myself getting madder the more I think about it. I look at him but he is smiling at me and his smile is so gorgeous I can't help but smile back.

"I know you want to say something Tasha, go on just say it." he has a little giggle. I don't know what's so funny.

"I can't believe a man of your age goes clubbing three times a week. I thought you worked too hard for that Caleb. I'm surprised that's all." I say and I can feel myself getting annoyed.

Caleb is just smiling at me and the other two are looking at me with their eyes wide. I suppose they're not used to me speaking my mind recently.

"Tasha I am past clubbing three times a week, you're right." he says.

"So what do you come here for three times a week? Is it for picking up women?" I don't know why I said that but my stomach is churning and it feels strange. I can feel myself getting angry but he just keeps smiling at me. Luca and Kammie are staring at me, I don't think they can quite believe it.

"Is that what you really think Tasha? That I come here to pick up women? I thought you might know me better than that." he isn't smiling anymore.

"Caleb I don't think that, I talk to you most nights so I know you don't do that. What else would you be doing Caleb?" I don't want to think about him and other women.

He smiles again and takes my hands in his, he is sat facing me and doesn't look away from me. "Tasha, the only reason I come here so often is because I own this club. This is one of the first businesses I bought. I don't want to sell it because it reminds me of where I started."

Oh my god I'm so embarrassed. "Caleb I'm so sorry I don't know why I said that to you but seriously I can't believe you own this club and I never knew. So that's how we jumped the queue and you didn't pay for drinks." everything starts to sink in now. I turn to Kammie and Luca. "Did you two know?"

"No way," says Luca, "I'd have come more often if I did." he laughs. Kammie just shakes her head.

"I'm sorry I didn't say anything Tasha

but it didn't really crop up. Now you know so let's move on and have a good night." He says releasing my hands.

"Ok boss." I say laughing and everyone else joins in with me. We sit and drink and laugh for another hour or so.

"Come on Kammie I want to dance some more, is that ok Caleb?" I ask.

"Tasha you don't need to ask me if you can dance, I love watching you dance." he smiles and when I stand up he reaches out and touches my leg, "Enjoy Tasha."

Me and Kammie go off to the dance floor leaving Luca and Caleb alone.

We strut our stuff and laugh for a long time. I can feel Caleb watching me and I dance even more sexually just for him. I know it's wrong but the drink and actually relaxing starts to take its toll. Next thing Luca and Caleb join us on the dance floor and we all follow the saying "Dance like nobody is watching" we all fall about the place laughing and then go back to our table.

"That was so much fun." Kammie says laughing.

"I know I haven't had fun like that for so long." I reply taking a big swig of my drink.

Caleb smiles and says, "You certainly looked like you were having fun Tasha, it's good to see you smiling, you're beautiful when you do!"

I smile at him and take his hand and hold it to my cheek and lean into it and say "Thanks Caleb that means a lot to me."

I'm embarrassed by his openness in front of Luca and Kammie but I don't need to worry, they are too busy kissing each other.

Caleb lowers his hand and rests it on my lap, he squeezes my leg and I look up at him and smile, he starts to lean forward and I think he's going to kiss me. I don't know how I feel about that in front of my friends. At the last minute he moves his head so that his mouth is by my ear, "Angel I want you so bad and I know I shouldn't but by god you're all I can think about. Dancing with you out there just makes me want you more, you are so sexy and beautiful and I thank god every day for bringing you into my life." he kisses me just below my ear on my neck and moans making the vibrations go through my body. I am so turned on right now and I know I shouldn't be but my body is betraying me. I moan too and he leans his head against my shoulder, "God Tasha, you are killing me right now." I don't know what to say, what do you say when someone says that to you.

"Caleb, let's go and dance now the music is slower, I want to hold you close." I say into his ear, he doesn't hesitate, he stands up and takes my hand.

"Guys we are off to dance, we'll catch you later, don't leave without us ok." Caleb says to the two of them.

He drags me to the back of the dance floor and asks the DJ to put on Fireflies by Owl City, I love this song. He takes me onto the dance floor. I lean into him and put my arms around his neck. "Caleb you feel so good." I think I'm really drunk, I don't say things like that to anyone.

He pulls me closer, "Not as good as you feel Tasha, I didn't think I would get to hold you this close, and now I can't stop, this is what I have been dreaming of."

We sway to the music and then to our own beat, it's like we are finding each other for the first time, I have never felt this turned on in my life, it is amazing, every beat is like Caleb is inside me, pounding into me.

"Caleb I want you to take me home."

"What now? Is this too much? Did I take it too far? Tasha?" he stops moving and just holds me. I can feel how much he wants me, his cock feels huge against my leg.

"No Caleb, I want to go home with you, I don't want tonight to end, please?" he pulls me closer, if that's possible.

"Do you feel how much I want you Tasha? I won't push you into anything you don't want, but if you're asking me to take you to my apartment then Tasha I will do what you want." he kisses me on the lips very gently and then starts to smile against my lips, it is so sexy.

"Come on Caleb, please, I want some alone time with you." I smile and grab his bum, god he has a sexy bum.

He takes my hand and he leads me over to our table where Kammie and Luca are eating each other. "Guys, we are off to mine if you want to come with us, we can finish the night there if you want." I appreciate him asking but I wanted to be alone with him. I start to pout, which isn't like me. He bends down and whispers in my ear, "I need your friends to like me and not to think I am taking advantage of you Tasha." I suppose I understand where he is coming from.

They both smile, "OK let's get out of here." Luca says, taking Kammie's hand and leading her out first.

10

I realise then that I don't know where Caleb's apartment is. "Is it far to go Caleb? I can't walk far in these heels." he laughs at me.

"No Tasha it's not far and if you struggle I'll just carry you." he kisses me on the cheek.

We walk two blocks and then we walk into a building which I thought was an office building, we walk past reception and Caleb says hello to the security guard.

We go into the lift and he presses the button for the penthouse, of course he does, why would he live anywhere else? I'm starting to realise how well off Caleb is, he doesn't come across as someone with a lot of money so I don't like to treat him as if he does.

When we get out of the lift we are inside the lounge area, it is amazing, so open plan and leads us straight to a floor to ceiling window which overlooks the whole of Bristol. "Wow Caleb, this is amazing, how do you ever leave this place to go to work?" Kammie says.

"Yeah mate, this is fabulous, do you have a balcony too?" Luca says walking towards the door that is hidden in the glass.

"Yeah of course I do." Caleb says, pulling me towards the window and opens the door and we all move outside to look at the view.

"Wow Caleb this is unbelievable, I have never seen anything so beautiful." I say.

"I have." Caleb says into my ear.

We all stand there looking out at the City of Bristol, not saying anything, then Caleb says, "Who wants a drink?" and he walks back into the apartment.

We all follow and he gets some glasses and drinks out for us all. After about half an hour, some food miraculously arrives, none of us ask any questions, we just eat. Then I start to feel sleepy, I know I have drunk more than I have drunk in a long time, Felix didn't really like me drinking so I never really did. I sit on the couch next to Caleb, lean against him and I can feel my eyes

getting heavy.

I can hear voices around me, "We should go home." Luca says.

"No stay, there are some spare rooms, you're more than welcome, I don't think Tasha can go home, so I'm sure her Mum would feel better if you stayed here as well tonight." Caleb says.

"OK," says Kammie, "you're a good guy Caleb, she's lucky to have you."

"No Kammie I'm lucky to have her in my life," Caleb replies. "She is everything I think about, I can't imagine my life without her, I can feel when she is hurting, why is that?"

"I don't know Caleb, but I think that maybe you are meant to be together and that has something to do with being soulmates. Me and Luca are soulmates, we need each other and I can't be without him because it hurts, so I know how you feel." Kammie replies, I didn't know this was how she felt about Luca, but I'm happy. I throw my arm around Caleb's middle and move in closer.

"I think she needs me too Kammie." Caleb says.

I drift off for a while and then I feel movement beneath me, what is happening?

"Tasha, I'm taking you to bed and I'm going to look after you ok?" What does he mean?

He lays me on the bed and asks where

my phone is. What a strange question. Next thing I know he is undressing me and then I feel something cold being put on me, I can feel a soft pillow beneath my head and I nuzzle in. This is so comfortable, I can hear Caleb moving around but my body feels so heavy I can feel myself drifting off.

I am vaguely aware of Caleb climbing in the bed behind me and pulling me close. He puts his arm around my stomach so that I am leaning into him and he whispers into my ear, "I think I'm falling in love with you Tasha, I don't think I would be happy without you. Stay with me always." I think that's what he said but I drift off. I must have imagined it.

11

When I wake up I look around me, where am I? Everything looks different, I slowly lift the covers to see if I'm naked, no I've got a t-shirt on but it's not mine. I can feel a heavy hand on my stomach and a leg draped across mine. What the heck! I slowly turn around to see who is in the bed with me. When I do I see the most beautiful sight in the world. Caleb is fast asleep, he moans in his sleep and pulls me closer. He only has a pair of shorts on him and I can see his chest, it's amazing it's so toned and bare.

"Morning Angel are you enjoying the view?" he says in a deep gravelly voice. He leans into me and kisses me on the forehead. I laugh.

"I can't believe I stayed here last night,

Mum will be so worried about me I have to go!" I start to panic.

"It's ok Tasha it's sorted, Kammie text her to let her know you were exhausted and fell asleep." he says pulling me in as close as he can. "I think I could get used to waking up with you next to me. What a great way to start the day."

I let him cuddle me because it feels so nice and so natural, I start to get hot and start wriggling to get out of his hold but when I do that I can feel his rock hard cock pushing in to me. I like that feeling.

After a few minutes Caleb says, "Come on Tasha let's get up and see how Kammie and Luca are, and before you ask we did nothing but sleep, ok. Yes, I undressed you and put my t-shirt on you but I didn't look." he has the biggest, stupidest grin on him.

"Liar!" I laugh because I know he did.

He rolls onto his back and starts laughing too. "Yeah I'm lying, but I just wanted to make you feel better."

I get out of the bed, "Where's the bathroom Caleb?" I really need to go.

He points to a door in his room and I walk over to it, all the time I can feel him looking at my legs. "Like what you see Caleb?" I know I'm flirting but I'm having fun.

When I come out of the bathroom the

bed is empty and the bedroom door is open.

I go towards the door and hear voices, "Seriously Caleb, you didn't take advantage of her last night did you?" it's Luca. "She's very vulnerable right now."

"Hey man what do you take me for, I have strong feelings for Tasha, I don't treat the connection we have lightly. When I make love to Tasha it will be when she is sober and the time is right. It isn't the right time now. Luca, I promise you that she is my forever." Caleb says. I don't listen to the rest because I am reeling with what I heard. He is such a wonderful man, I don't deserve him. Kammie comes up behind me, "Morning bitch how's the head?"

"Actually, it's not bad considering how much we drank. How's yours?"

"It's ok, thank god. Did you get a shock this morning when you realised you weren't alone in bed?" She's laughing because she knows I've never done the whole "one night stand" thing.

"I wasn't frightened because I just had a feeling of being safe. But I'd be lying if I said I didn't enjoy waking up to see a half-naked Caleb behind me." I start laughing and she joins in. We head down the stairs and the two guys look up and see us. They both start smiling and walking towards us.

Luca kisses Kammie on the lips, "Morning beautiful."

"You know that t-shirt looks better on you than it ever did on me?" Caleb smiles and takes my hand, "Come on let's get breakfast," and he leads the way to the kitchen. "So what does everyone want?" Caleb says going over to the coffee machine and turning it on. "Does anyone want a traditional fry up?"

We all start nodding and saying yeah. I go over to help him, "Sit Tasha, I like cooking for you." so I sit.

We all sit there and talk about the fun we had last night and then, "I just realised I didn't show you around the apartment, but I guess you've seen most of it. The only room you haven't seen is my office and that's really boring."

"Can we go and explore Caleb? Is your office out of bounds? or can we check each room out? Me and Kammie are nosey." I start to laugh and Kammie links arms with me.

"Tasha, nothing is out of bounds to you, what you see is what you get with me." we go off to explore. We walk through the lounge and out onto the balcony again, the view seems so different today in the light, but it is still spectacular.

"Wow Tasha, imagine waking up to this view every day, it's amazing." Kammie says.

"I know, you should see the view at his

beach house, that's even more beautiful." I say with a smile.

We go upstairs and I show Kammie the master bedroom, I didn't have a good look around earlier, I was too busy checking Caleb out. It is fabulous, the bed is huge, the biggest I've ever seen and again the wardrobes are hidden in the wall and we look out the floor to ceiling window showing another view of the city.

We check out the other bedrooms, they are all nice but nothing like the master bedroom, we go back downstairs and find the office, Caleb was right it is boring.

We go back into the kitchen to find the boys talking and laying the table, I could get used to this. "Hey did you find anything interesting when you were looking around?" Caleb says.

"No, but everything is beautiful, is that breakfast I can smell, is it ready? I'm starving." I say.

"Yes it is, go and sit down, Tasha will you help me bring the plates in?" he says.

"Yes of course I will." I say going further into the kitchen.

When I go to lift the plates to take them in, Caleb stops me, "Tasha I just wanted to say good morning properly," and he leans in and kisses me on the lips, he pulls my body into his and I can feel my hands reaching up to his head to push him closer, I know I shouldn't be doing this but I can't help myself. I can feel his tongue invading my mouth and I don't want to do anything to stop it. My tongue can't get enough of his mouth, I pull back slightly and take his lower lip between my teeth and suck gently.

He groans and puts his hands on my arse and pushes me closer to him, he stops kissing me and pulls back slightly, "Good morning, now I could do that every day. You are so gorgeous. Now you need to go and take the plates in I can't move for a few minutes," as he's saying this I can feel his cock twitch against me so I definitely know what he means. I can feel myself blushing because I did that to him. I stand back and take a look down his body and I can see the outline of his cock and I gasp and then look back up to him. He's smiling, "You did that to me Tasha, it's all yours but not here and not today."

I blush again and then take the plates through to the dining area. Luca and Kammie look at me. "Was it hot in the kitchen Tasha you're all red." Luca says laughing and that makes me blush even more.

I sit in my seat and it's another couple of minutes before Caleb comes through with the rest of the plates. I smile at him and Luca starts giggling, "Warm enough for you Caleb?"

Caleb just starts laughing, "Shut up Luca." we all join in. This is so relaxed I don't think I ever had this much fun when Felix was with us all. I try not to think about it because I'm enjoying myself for the first time in a long time.

12

After breakfast me and Kammie do the dishes and clear up and then go out to the balcony where the boys are. "What are everyone's plans for the day?" Kammie says sitting on Luca's lap.

Everyone shakes their heads because no one has much in mind. "I have to go home and get changed." I say laughing.

"Why? You look good in my t-shirt." Caleb says pulling me close to him.

"I can't walk around in your t-shirt all day Caleb." I say laughing at him.

"Well, for me you could Tasha." he smiles back.

"I think I need to go home and show Mum and Dad that I'm alive, it's strange after being able to do what I want when I want, to have to answer to them again. I don't think they expect me to, but I am staying in their house and I respect them." I say a little sadly.

"What is happening with the house Tasha?" Kammie asks.

"I've put it on the market, I don't want to move back in, there are too many memories and not all of them are good. So I'm staying with Mum and Dad until it's all finalised and then I can start looking at where I go next." I don't really know if I can stay in Mum's for too much longer without being stifled.

"I have a couple of apartments Tasha that you could rent if you want to get your freedom back, you know that." Caleb says, he's so thoughtful.

I reach out and touch my hand on his arm, "Thanks Caleb, I might take you up on the offer." he smiles a really wide smile.

"Anytime Tasha, anytime." I can see Kammie smiling at me, I know she can't believe how good he is to me, but I think she likes him and she likes me being with him.

"I'd like to do something fun today, anyone up for that." I say, "but I can't be too late home because I have to start my new job tomorrow."

I look up at Caleb and smile, he smiles

back, "I hear your new boss is a tyrant." He laughs.

"What about going to Millennium Square and ice skating?" Luca says, I'm surprised, it's not really a manly sport.

Kammie starts jumping up and down, "Yeah lets, yeah." Now I know why he said it, I laugh.

"Caleb, do you want to do that or do you have work to do today?" I ask him, I want him to come with us, I don't want this weekend to end, it's been amazing.

"Do you guys mind me tagging along, I'd love to go with you but I don't want to put you all out." he says.

"Come on Caleb I don't want to be the only bloke there and having the girls laugh at me, of course we want you to come." Luca says going over to him and patting him on the shoulder. I must remember to say thank you to Luca later, he's making Caleb feel very welcome considering the circumstances. Felix was Luca's best friend for many years, I know it must be hard to see me being so friendly with Caleb so quickly, but to me it feels right.

"OK, then I'll come with you and see who can fall the most." he laughs.

We all go upstairs to get dressed, I don't want to do the walk of shame in my dress from last night so Caleb lends me his t-shirt and some tracksuit bottoms. I feel so unsexy, but I just need to get home and put some of my clothes on. The thought that Caleb has been wearing these clothes makes me hug them closer to me.

"Tasha I have to say there is something sexy about you wearing my clothes, I won't wash them again if it means that I can smell you on them," he leans forward and kisses me on the forehead. "Come on let's get out of here before I try to make you stay." he winks at me, I laugh.

Caleb drives Kammie and Luca to Luca's place and then drives on to my Mum's. He comes to the front door with me, "Tasha thank you for last night, I'm really glad I bumped into you, and I loved waking up with you in my bed." he's whispering in my ear so that Mum can't hear him, "I want to do it every day." he kisses me on the cheek and then stands up as Mum opens the door. "I'm sorry about last night Jean, Tasha was exhausted and then when the others were going to go home she had fallen asleep, they all stayed at mine for the night. I assume you got the text."

"Yes I did thank you Caleb, it's fine I was hoping Tasha would enjoy herself, she needed a bit of fun." Mum says.

"Well, we are going ice skating in a while so she's just come home to get changed." he smiles at Mum.

"Ice skating, that should be interesting."

Mum says smiling, "Come on in then, you can wait for her while she gets changed, I assume you're not staying in those clothes Tasha?"

"No definitely not, I'll go upstairs now and get changed." I'm not sure I want to leave them alone, this feels quite awkward.

I go upstairs and change really quickly into something more suitable for ice skating. When I come down the stairs I can't see anyone but I can hear them in the kitchen. "So Caleb," it's Dad, "Tasha is really vulnerable right now and I would hate to think of you taking advantage of that fact, she has been through so much and I don't want her to hurt any more than she already has." Wow go Dad!

"Sir I have feelings for Tasha that I can't explain, I have never had them before, I want to protect her from any hurt, from everything. I know what she has been through and it's been tough, but as long as she wants me to be in her life in whatever capacity, I will make sure that she stays happy and doesn't get hurt." I don't want to walk in because I have tears in my eyes, he is so perfect!

"Ok son, I know you won't hurt her and I know you will look after her, you're welcome here anytime." I can hear Dad move towards Caleb and take him in a hug and slap him on the shoulder.

I wait a couple of minutes and then I walk into the kitchen, they are all stood around with their cups of coffee and all look guilty like they were caught out, which I suppose they were.

"Are you ready Caleb? We should go, Kammie and Luca will be nearly there." I smile at Mum who nods her head at me.

Caleb follows me out to the front door and then we both turn and say goodbye. "Sir, I'll have her home early as she is starting her new job tomorrow and she will need to have a good sleep." Dad nods his head at him and smiles.

When we are in the car and driving away from the house, I say, "Caleb I heard what you said to my Dad, did you mean it?"

He reaches over and takes my hand, he brings it to his mouth and kisses it, "Every single word of it Tasha and more, I don't want to scare you with my feelings, but I intend to be around for a long time." he places my hand back onto my leg and then leaves his hand on top of it.

"What did I do to deserve someone like you Caleb?" I ask him because I just don't know.

"Because you're you Angel," and that's all he says.

13

We drive the rest of the way in silence, we don't need to say anything, his fingers keep rubbing my hand.

When we park and go to the ice rink we see Luca and Kammie straight away, they are in the queue, they wave us over. We go get our skates and put them on, then we walk to the ice and get on. It's been ages since I've been ice skating, I used to love the feeling of the wind blowing on my face as I skated around. I look at Caleb and start laughing, he can hardly stand up. "Caleb are you ok?"

"Yeah, I just ... I haven't skated before, I'll be fine, just go off and do your thing." he says holding onto the barrier all the way round.

It was all going well, until Caleb fell, he was flat out on the ice. I heard him go down and rushed over to him, I slid on the ice and was at his side. "Caleb are you ok? Are you hurt? Answer me." I touch his face and then I start checking the rest of his body to make sure he is ok.

"I'm fine Tasha, honestly I just banged my head." he laughs and sits up. I stand up and pull him to his feet. He stumbles a little and has to hold onto me to steady himself, he puts his arm around me at the same time and pulls me in close. "Were you worried about me? You rushed over. Maybe you do care about me after all." he has the biggest smile.

I lean into his hug and whisper in his ear, "You know I care about you, more than I should and I can't change that." I laugh into his ear and he pulls me in closer if that is possible and whispers in my ear "I don't think you know how much I care about you but I know how much I want to show you."

I pull back and I am greeted by the biggest smile I have ever seen and I can feel my panties getting wet. I try to cross my legs but it doesn't help matters. I laugh and blush at the same time.

Caleb laughs too and I skate off, he tries to follow me, but he isn't as good a skater as me. This is fun, I'm laughing and smiling and having fun and it seems like a lot has happened since I last had so much fun.

We skate for an hour then we go over to the Little Cozy Place coffee shop and have a hot chocolate. We sit at a table and me and Kammie sit on one side and Luca and Caleb on the other side. We don't talk when we drink our hot chocolate and warm our hands on our mugs. I can't stop staring at Caleb he is so handsome I just want to lean across and kiss him but I can't do that, it isn't right, but god I want to taste his sweet lips and have his hands touching my body.

"Tasha, hello are you with us?" Kammie asks laughing.

"Sorry I was miles away." I smiled.

We all laugh, it has been such a fun day. Luca and Kammie stay in town as they are going to go out for dinner later. They seem to be really getting on well and I'm so happy for them, they are two people who deserve happiness in their lives and I'm glad they found it together.

Caleb takes me home before dinner time so that I can rest before my big day tomorrow. He hugs me when he says goodbye and kisses me on the cheek, I feel like we are getting closer. The thought scares me and excites me at the same time.

I had so much fun this weekend, I felt alive for the first time in years if I'm truthful with myself. I sit down and tell Mum and Dad about the ice skating and what a fun day we had.

"Well I have to say Tasha, you look so healthy from the exercise and the fresh air. You look happy and it makes us happy to see you like that." Mum says smiling at me.

We play cards and I beat the two of them, it feels like Christmas, I love it. This is the best way to spend a Sunday evening, nice and relaxed before I start my new job.

It's about 10pm when I decide to go to bed, I want to talk to Caleb before I go to sleep. "Night Mum, night Dad I'm going to bed, I need my beauty sleep for tomorrow." I go over and give them both a kiss on the cheek.

"Night baby girl, I'm so excited for your new adventure tomorrow." mum says smiling at me.

I walk upstairs and get ready for bed, when I'm settled under the covers I ring Caleb, I don't just want to text him tonight, I feel like I need to hear his voice.

"Hey Caleb are you busy?"

"Tasha I'm never too busy to talk to you."

"I wanted to ring you tonight and not just text you, I needed to hear your voice."

"I'm glad you did, I love hearing yours too."

"I'm nervous about tomorrow Caleb and I'm excited too."

"There's no need to be nervous Angel, you are good at what you do and you will be fine. Thank you for a fabulous weekend, I loved every minute of it but there were some moments that I enjoyed more." I can hear the smile in his voice.

"Me too, I just wanted to tell you that I kept your clothes and I'm wearing them now in bed, they smell of you. I know it will help me to sleep."

"I can't believe you stole my clothes," he laughs. "I can just imagine you wearing them Angel, you looked so good wearing them this morning." he groans. "I'm in bed too and I was thinking about you, I'm so glad you rang me."

Neither of us say anything for a couple of minutes, then I say, "Caleb, thank you."

"What for Angel?"

"For being you. For being in my life."

"It's me that needs to thank you Tasha for being in my life, you've brought me meaning to my life. It was work, work, work before and now even that isn't as important to me as you are."

"Wow, talking about work, I need to go I have a new job to start tomorrow."

"Ok Tasha, sleep well and see you tomorrow bright and early."

"Night night Caleb, thanks for a great

............"

"Tasha, are you ok? Tasha ….. guess you must have fallen asleep on me. Hope you sleep well Angel, I'm so happy you came into my life. I know I can make you happy, I know I'm falling hard for you and I hope you are too. I'm going to end this call now Angel, it's going to be a busy week for both of us."

14

How did I get into this situation? Felix is dead, so why is he in my room hitting me? Why am I in the corner of the room while he kicks me? It hurts so much, I thought this was over!

I'm shouting at him to stop, "Felix please stop, you don't want to do this."

He stops kicking me and he spits on me, "You had fun this weekend Tasha, this is what happens when I don't remind you that you're mine. You shouldn't be having fun Tasha not without me."

I cower in the corner and I shout at him again, "Felix you're dead leave me alone, I need to move on and so do you. You made me so unhappy towards the end, I need to be happy, please leave me alone." I know I'm crying.

All of a sudden I hear my door bang open and Dad is in front of me, "Baby girl I'm here I will look after you, it's ok."

I wake up and just stare at Dad, then I fall into his arms and cry like a baby. "Why Dad? Why tonight? Is it because I had so much fun? Should I not be having fun anymore?"

"Tasha don't be silly, it's your subconscious that's all, yes you should be having fun, don't let Felix hurt you anymore baby girl, please." he hugs me some more and I can feel myself drifting off to sleep.

15

When I wake up, I'm in my bed. I must have just dreamt it all and Dad didn't come into me.

Today is my first day at my new job, I'm nervous for a few reasons, because it's a new company, it's my first time back at work since Felix passed away and lastly because of Caleb - I don't want anyone to know that we are friends outside work. I explained this to Caleb and he doesn't see it as a problem, but I pleaded with him until he relented and agreed, although he told me that he wouldn't lie if someone asked him about me.

That was good enough for me and I agreed with him, he then said that he would let me get settled in but in six months' time he hoped he would be able to freely tell people that we were friends. I agreed to the six months' time limit, it gave me enough time to show my colleagues who I am and what I am capable of before they know about our friendship.

When I arrive at work, I'm reintroduced to Helen from HR and shown around the office, she introduced me to loads of people who I'll never remember. I'm shown my office, it's gorgeous, the desk is in front of a large picture window looking over the townscape of Bristol, I can see I'll be looking out the window a lot.

I turn my computer on, I have an appointment with Steve in 5 minutes. He's one of the IT guys and he is going to set me up with usernames and show me the internal systems that they use. I love computers so I'm looking forward to it.

Steve is a lovely guy, he made me feel at home and not out of place at all. He is really funny and I find myself relaxing with him. It turns out he's gay and we spend quite a lot of time talking about his relationship problems. I've laughed so much my stomach hurts.

He sits with me and goes over all the procedures and computer programmes for about 3 hours and then it's lunch time. I'm thinking about what to do for lunch when Meg, the receptionist, comes into my office and asks me if I want to go to the canteen with her and Steve. I agree and they show me where it is.

When we are sitting at our table they both start talking at once, I start laughing and then we all fall around laughing. This is a great first day!

After lunch I go back to my office and check my emails. There is one from Caleb, it's all business-like and it feels strange. I suppose this is the email that gets sent to all new starters. As I'm reading it I get a text.

"Hey Tasha I hope you're settling in ok. Sorry I'm not there today I have meetings, I will be back later but it will be much later on."

"It's no problem Caleb it's probably better you're not here today."

"I have a strange week at work this week so I'll be in and out of the office. I want to see you though, maybe we can go to dinner on Wednesday after work"

"I'd love that Caleb. I'm so excited about this job but I was secretly hoping to see you"

"I'd see you all the time if I could Angel you know that"

"I know Caleb, I know ;-)"

Since I've heard from him and know he's not going to be here today, I relax and start going through some of the tasks that Steve left me.

There's a knock on my door at 5.15pm, it's Meg. "Hi Natasha, everyone's gone home I just wanted to make sure you're ok?" she smiles at me.

"Gosh I didn't realise the time, yeah I'm fine. Just trying to read up on everything we do here."

"I'll walk with you so we can chat about your day." she says passing me my jacket.

I like her she's so kind, "Thanks Meg." I say as I'm packing my bag and putting my jacket on.

We walk out together and talk about my day. Meg tells me she's only new herself but she had temped here for a while and that she was only just made permanent recently.

We say goodbye when we get to the car park and she says she will see me in the morning. I drive home and Mum and Dad are waiting for me to tell them how I got on.

I'm so excited that I know I'm rambling and not taking a breath, mum laughs.

"Tasha take a breath we've got all night you know." she starts laughing and so do Dad and I.

"I know it's just it was exciting and strange at the same time. Everyone was really nice, especially Steve and Meg, they made me feel very welcome."

"Tasha you look happy, I'm glad you're excited." Dad says smiling.

Kammie and Luca both ring me to see how I got on and I know they are happy for me.

When I go to bed I get a text from Caleb.

"Hey how did your first day go?"

"Hi boss lol it went well, everyone is so nice. I had lunch with Meg and Steve ☺"

"Good I'm glad you had someone to go to lunch with. Everyone's very good with new people. I'm glad you're happy Tasha"

"Thanks Caleb, I had a bad nightmare last night, I think it was because I had so much fun over the weekend with you"

"Are you ok? Were you ok? I wish I could have been there to look after you"

"I wish you were too"

I can't believe I just said that, but it's true.

"Angel I'd be there every night if I could xx"

"I know and I know you'd keep me safe Caleb, you already do x"

"Good then I'm doing my job ☺ I want to look after you and make all your pain go away xx"

"Thank you. Now I have to get up early for work tomorrow, so I have to sleep"

"Ok see you soon Angel, I hope you sleep well tonight xx"

I lay looking at ceiling for a while just thinking about my day, about Caleb and my new friends. I fall asleep smiling.

16

The next day at work there are a couple of meetings I have to attend, I was hoping Caleb would be in them, but he's not, I think he might be avoiding me. I text him after lunch.

"Are you avoiding me? Everyone tells me you usually meet new people on the first day ☺"

"No I'm not avoiding you Angel, my body is craving you. Believe you me, I would love nothing better than to come and see you and say hi. It's just there are problems on an account that I need to deal with but we are having dinner tomorrow aren't we?"

"I was only joking with you Caleb. I now

you wouldn't avoid me. Yes we are having dinner tomorrow. I need to see you too x"

"Good now get back to work ha ha xx"

On Wednesday I don't see him all day again, he sends me a text in the afternoon.

"I'll collect you from your Mums around 7.30 pm is that ok?"

"Yeah that's fine. I can't wait to see you Caleb"

"I know the feeling Angel. See you soon xx"

When I get home from work I go and take a shower and start getting ready for Caleb. I'm really excited about dinner, I can't wait to see him. I put on a dress because I don't know where we are going.

The bell rings bang on 7.30pm and I go to open the door. As my hand reaches for the door I take a deep breath to try and still my erratic heart. I open it slowly and when I see him standing there in front of me I can't speak or breathe, he is just so gorgeous he literally took my breath away.

I come to my sense when I hear, "Tasha, are you ok? Breathe Angel, Breathe."

I take a big gulp in, "Sorry Caleb I don't know what happened there." I blush I'm embarrassed.

He smiles and gives me a hug and whispers in my ear, "I feel the same Angel." he knows I'm overwhelmed.

I smile at him when he pulls away from me, he leans forward and shouts through the door, "Hi Jean, Hi Brian." They reply back and tell us both to enjoy our night.

"Come on then let's go Tasha." he says holding out his hand for me to take.

I take it and smile at him, I close the door behind me and he walks me to the car. As usual he opens the door and waits for me to buckle up before he goes around to his side of the car.

When he's driving I ask where we are going.

"We are going to a lovely little restaurant I know in Bath, is that ok? I know it's an hour drive but I promise you it's worth it." he smiles and I would do anything he asks me to do just to see that smile.

I reach over and take his hand off the gear stick and place it in between mine, "Caleb that's fine I don't mind how far away it is. I'm just so excited to be with you."

He turns my hand so that he is holding mine and then he takes it up to his mouth and kisses it gently.

"So tell me about work Tasha. How have you got on?"

I sit for the whole journey telling him about what I've been doing and how I've had meetings with the admin staff trying to find out what they do and how we can make improvements. He smiles and asks questions and it all feels so natural and relaxing.

When we pull up to the restaurant it's beautiful, I've always loved Bath and am so excited to be here.

Over dinner we talk about the weekend and how much fun we had ice skating. I love being in his company, he is entertaining, interesting and very easy on the eye. I giggle to myself.

"What are you laughing at Tasha?" he says staring into my eyes. I start to blush and he starts to smile.

"I was thinking how much fun tonight has been and how gorgeous you are," the wine must have gone to my head.

He looks at me then he starts laughing and he's even better looking when he does that. "Tasha you always surprise me. You never say what I expect you to say! I'm glad you're having fun. So am I."

We manage to get through dinner without any more outbursts from me. When it's time to go, Caleb pays the bill and he takes my hand and we walk outside to the car. As we get closer to the car he pulls me into him by my shoulders, "Tasha I really enjoyed tonight, I don't want it to end, is that bad of me?"

"No Caleb I don't want it to end either." as the last word leaves my mouth he has turned me and pushed me up against the car and his lips are on mine.

He groans and then he says, "God I want you so much," into my mouth. My hands have moved into his hair and I pull him closer to me. I want him too, I feel like I need him.

After a while he pulls away, I'm glad because I don't think I have the strength to. I feel weak all over.

"Come on Angel before this gets out of hand, that's not what I want for you and me. I want to wait until you're ready and until you want all of me."

What does he mean by that? I don't understand.

"Ok Caleb, but you'll have to explain that because I don't understand." he takes my hand and walks me to the door, opens it and waits until my seatbelt is on before going to his side and sliding into his seat.

"Ok just hear me out please," I nod and he carries on, "we both know we have a connection," I nod again. "I don't want to have sex with you Tasha that's not what this is about." I can feel tears welling up in my eyes. I reach for the door handle but he takes my hand gently.

"Tasha you promised to hear me out. I want to make love to you not just have sex, I want a relationship with you not just a fling, a rebound. I want you to want me so much that it is all you can think about because that's how I feel about you. I want you to feel what I feel and I don't think you're ready yet. I could try and have sex with you now and it could set you back months, even years. I don't want that for you Tasha, I want everything with you!"

I stare straight ahead, I can't look at him.

"Tasha, why're you crying?" He looks so sad.

"Caleb I want all that, I want everything, I just don't know if I can give you that right now. My body and mind say yes but my heart isn't sure."

"I know Angel that's why I stopped, it doesn't mean I care any less. I'm not going anywhere, you are well worth the wait." he leans across and kisses me gently on the lips. This kiss feels more emotional than the last one.

"Thank you Caleb for being you."

He smiles at me and then starts the car. On the drive home we talk about my house and whether I want to move into one of his apartments or not. I tell him I'm not ready to be on my own yet because I still keep having nightmares. I can see he gets sad when I tell him about my nightmares, "I'd do anything to stop those for you Angel I really would."

"I know Caleb, hopefully they'll start to lessen soon." I say sadly.

"Now let's not get sad, we had a great night and I want to do it again soon." he smiles.

"Me too." I smile back.

He drops me home and walks me to the door. He leans down and kisses me on the lips, "I love the taste of your lips Tasha."

I laugh. "That's because they taste of wine and you couldn't drink tonight." I laugh and he laughs too.

"No Tasha, that's because they taste of you. I'm going to have to drag myself away. I had a great night see you at work," he gives me a quick kiss on the cheek, then he turns and walks back to the car. He waits till I close the door behind me before he drives off.

Mum and dad are in bed so I go straight upstairs and get ready for bed. When I climb under the covers I smile to myself, I'm so lucky to have Caleb in my life.

17

Friday comes around quick and I'm looking forward to work, it's dress down day so I'm wearing my jeans in. Apparently everyone goes to The Angel pub after work for a few drinks on a Friday. Caleb is supposed to go as he always buys everyone a drink. It should be interesting!

There's quite a few people there and I see that there's a couple of people who I haven't met yet and I am quickly introduced to them. They are all very friendly and some of them are very good looking, Meg really likes one of them, Dillon. He's the Operations Manager who interviewed me. I am talking to him and he keeps looking at me funny, he is starting to creep me out. "So Natasha, how has your first week with us been?"

"I've really enjoyed being here, everyone is so nice and friendly. I don't think I've met everyone yet though, there are so many people working here. How long have you worked in the Company, Dillon?" I ask him.

He smiles at me with a million dollar smile. "I've worked with Caleb since he started the company. We're best friends!"

He looks into my eyes and smiles and says, "I think we've met before your interview actually in Jesters a couple of months ago."

I blush when I realise he was the man that was with Caleb that fateful night when my life started going wrong. "I'm sorry I don't remember seeing you, I was too busy trying to clean up my drink off Caleb." I give a small giggle and look up to see he is smiling at me.

He leans forward and whispers in my ear "Angel? Isn't it? The woman who has stolen Caleb's heart." I gasp when he says it and pull back to look at him.

"Is that a problem?" I ask, not feeling sure of myself.

"Not at all Tasha, I'm delighted, he is a much better man for having met you, and seeing you here tonight I can see what he adores about you. Now I'm going to buy a drink because Meg is giving you the evils and I know you don't need that hassle after your first week." he nods his head to Meg and then walks to the bar.

I stand there and stare after him then turn and walk back to Meg, "I can see why you like him! Shame I'm not in the market for a man right now." I start to giggle and Meg laughs along with me, we are going to be great friends.

"He is damn fine isn't he?" she says eying him all the time, when he turns away from the bar and starts to walk up to her she starts to blush.

"I'll leave you two alone for a while." I say walking away to another group of work colleagues. After an hour my phone rings and I can see it is Caleb calling.

"Hey Tasha, how are you doing after your first week at work? Are you in the pub celebrating?" he says.

"Hiya, yeah I'm in The Angel pub next door to the office, I just met Dillon, again!" I laugh remembering how I met him the first time.

"Ah yeah, I forgot to mention that," he laughs, "Would you be embarrassed if I joined you all for a drink, I usually do." I can tell he wanted to give me some space, but he doesn't want to do something that is different to normal.

"Of course it's fine, it might feel awkward, but I'm sure we can control ourselves." I laugh.

"Speak for yourself," he says, laughing. "I'll be there in 10 minutes so prepare yourself," and he hangs up.

I take a deep breath and walk over to Tracey, she is one of the secretaries who has been good to me this week. "Thanks for helping me get through my first week, you've been a great help. How long have you worked here?" we stand talking for ten minutes or more and then I can feel Caleb behind me, he doesn't need to speak or do anything, I just know he's there.

"Mr Hunt it's great to see you tonight, didn't think you were going to come along, thought you might have been busy." Tracey says giving him a big smile.

"I had to come and see my new employee and see how her first week went, you know the drill," he laughs. "So T.. Natasha, how was your first week at work?"

I turn to talk to Caleb and falter at my first sight of him, "Mr Hunt, it's a pleasure." I say sticking my hand out for him to shake. Big mistake because he takes my hand and shakes it and then rubs his thumb under my wrist. I can feel myself getting flustered and so I take my hand away quickly. He looks at me and hides his smile. "I've really enjoyed this week, everyone has been really friendly and I'm starting to settle in."

"That's great news, I've heard good

reports from everyone so far. Now that I've let you settle in this week, I have some projects I want you to work on starting next week. We can talk about them on Monday morning so don't worry about them now. Do you want a drink? I usually buy a round for everyone on a Friday?" he asks walking towards the bar.

I turn to look at Tracey, "Does he really do that? That's really cool." she laughs and nods her head. I follow Caleb to the bar, "Mr Hunt I'd love a drink, can I have a coke, I have to drive home tonight."

He turns and smiles at me and leans into me and says, "I'll make sure you get home Tasha, have a proper drink," and then he stands up and orders a vodka to go in my coke.

I take my drink, say thanks and then walk around talking to everyone for a while. After about 20 minutes I get a text from Caleb.

"I want you to know how much I like you calling me Mr Hunt LOL"

"Well it is your name Mr Hunt!!!"

"Yeah I know, but it turns me on Tasha"

"OMG Caleb you didn't just say that to me did you?"

"Yeah I think I did Natasha, what are

you going to do about it?"

I don't reply, I walk over to him and say, "Mr Hunt, thank you so much for my drink, I was wondering if I can buy you a drink back Mr Hunt. What do you drink Mr Hunt?" I am trying so hard not to laugh because his face is hilarious.

He stutters, "Thank you Natasha that would be very kind. I'll have a long sloe screw please."

That's it for me I start laughing so hard and I can feel tears coming down my face. "You did not just say that did you Mr Hunt?" I say between laughs.

He laughs in return and says, "Now Natasha do you need me to repeat that or have you heard of it before?"

I turn from him and go up to the bar and ask the barman for a long sloe screw, laughing all the time. My phone beeps with another message.

"This is so hard Tasha, all I want to do is hold you in my arms and kiss you, you need to stop laughing you look so beautiful"

I smile while I read the message and then I turn around to see the most handsome face looking at me, smiling. He starts to walk towards me and I know, I just know that he doesn't want to wait 6 months, he wants to do it now. I start shaking my head because I need to wait longer, I need to get to know these people and let them get to know me. He stops and the smile falls off his face and I feel sad that I did that to him. I walk over to him and hand him his drink and say, "Sorry Caleb I can't do it now," and then I go over to Tracey and Meg and say goodnight. I know Caleb can't follow me because it would look too strange to the others.

I stand outside the pub and lean against the wall, I'm breathing heavily, I feel like crying, Caleb looked so hurt and I don't want to hurt him. I know he won't follow me, he wants me to have some space to think about what happened.

I'm confused, I want to go back and tell him I'm sorry and show everyone how much he means to me, but I can't do it. I don't know if I can let myself get into a relationship again and be hurt. How can I trust him to be himself? What if he's only pretending too? I don't know if I can trust my heart to anyone again.

I sink to the floor and start sobbing, I feel someone walk up to me and sink to the ground with me. It's Dillon!

"He sent me out to make sure you're ok, he's frantic he can't just walk out. Too many people would ask questions and you don't want that. Caleb has told me about what happened to you and how he's been there for you and I admire him. It's hard to be in love with someone who doesn't love you back Tasha. I've never seen Caleb like this with anyone, you're everything he thinks about, talks about and dreams about. I just hope you're worth it, because right now I don't think you are! To hurt him like you just did," he reaches out and takes my hand in his. "Tasha that man in there was prepared to lay his heart down in front of people who respect him and you hurt him, you threw it back at him. I know he said he would wait 6 months but I really don't think he can. He needs to know how you feel and he needs to know tonight. I'm going back in so think about it seriously Tasha. You'll always have a job here but you need to make your mind up. Do you want Caleb the way he wants you or what do you want?"

Before he stands up and leaves me I say, "Dillon you said you know what I've been through, you know I've had my heart ripped out and stamped on. I'm not sure I can do that to myself again Dillon." I wipe the tears away from my face. "I know I have strong feelings for Caleb and I can feel myself falling in love with him, I just don't know if I can let go of that last bit of my heart."

"Tasha I understand that, but in my opinion no one will ever love you or treat you any better than Caleb Hunt. He wears his heart on his sleeve and he wants your heart in return" now I'm going in for another drink are you going to join me?" He holds his hand out for me to take to pull myself up, I reach out and take his hand. He pulls me close and hugs me. "He's worth everything and more Tasha take a chance."

I step back and look at him and smile. "Will you promise to be there to pick up the pieces of my heart if he breaks it?"

I look up into Dillon's eyes and see him smile, "I promise I will beat him up myself if he does." he holds his arm out for me to take and after two beats of my heart I slide my arm through his. He smiles and just like his best friend he has a gorgeous smile. We walk thought the door and Caleb turns around and smiles when he sees me, thank god I didn't piss him off too much. Dillon walks straight over to him and the group of people he is standing with. "Look who I found outside who couldn't get a taxi. I talked her into coming in for another drink." Everyone welcomes me back and they keep on talking.

All the time Caleb is watching me, waiting for me to be on my own so he can talk to me. I know what I need to do, I just need to build up the courage to do it, to take what I want and not be afraid of the consequences. I take a few deep breaths and slowly walk over to him, I can see him staring at me and looking around him to see who is watching, he doesn't know what to expect from me. Neither do I!

When I'm stood in front of him I slowly raise my head to look at him and I say, "Mr Hunt, Caleb can I ask you something?"

He's nodding his head. "Yes of course you can." he says uncertainly.

I reach up and pull his head down to mine, "Can I kiss you?" I say and don't wait for an answer, I put my lips over his very gently and then a little harder, all the time I am looking him in the eye and I can see them widen with shock.

He starts to return the kiss and puts his arms around me and pulls me close, he groans into my mouth, "Tasha, my Angel."

After what seems like an hour we pull apart and I just smile at him. Everyone is looking at us and I start to blush, I don't know what to say. Caleb pulls me into him by the shoulder and says, "Everyone I want to introduce you to my girlfriend Tasha, she didn't want you to know because she doesn't want you to judge her but I can't hide it when I'm around her." he kisses me on the side of my head and smiles at me. I just want to curl up and die.

Dillon comes over and claps Caleb on the shoulder and then comes over and kisses me on the cheek. "You did the right thing Tasha."

Everyone else starts congratulating Caleb and smiling at me. Caleb goes and buys me a drink and Tracey comes over to me, "You sly dog," she says, "we've all wanted a piece of his ass for a long time, but I can see how happy he has been for a while now. Congratulations Natasha."

I smile and hug her "Thanks Tracey, I wanted you all to know that I got this job because of me and my skills not because of Caleb."

"Oh we know that honey, you're whipping us into shape already." she laughs.

Caleb comes back to me and gives me my drink. "What changed your mind Tasha?"

"Dillon had a little word with me and promised me that he would beat you up if you broke my heart," I laugh and reach up and kiss him gently on the lips. "Can we get out of here soon? I think we need to talk?" I ask.

"Anything for you, my Angel, anything."

"Ok, then I want you to take me back to your apartment and let me stand on your balcony while you wrap your arms around me and hold me tight." I smile.

"Ok down your drink we're leaving now." he laughs. "Dillon, thanks buddy for talking to Tasha, now we have some things to talk about so we are going to leave, make sure you buy everyone a couple of drinks, I'm feeling generous all of a sudden." Oh my god I love that smile.

"See you Monday morning bright and early everyone, me and Tasha are off now, enjoy your evening, Dillon will get a couple of rounds in for you, night." Everyone starts talking at once, "thanks" "cheers" "behave" Caleb laughs as he takes my hand and we leave the pub.

When we get outside he turns and says, "Are you sure about this Tasha?" and then he leans up against me and kisses me like his life depends on it.

"Tasha I'll give you whatever you want, you've made me so happy tonight." he kisses me so deeply I feel like I'm going to explode.

We walk back to his apartment holding hands and every now and again we stop and kiss, because we can. I know I have a big smile on my face, but I can't help it I have this beautiful man kissing me.

When we get back to his apartment we get into the lift and he pushes me against the wall very gently, he doesn't want to frighten me, he puts his two hands above my head and he bends down slightly so that he can kiss me. "I can't get enough of your lips Tasha, now that you've allowed me to have them I can never give them up. They are beautiful and taste divine." he says as he plunges his tongue into my mouth. He is such a great kisser I think I can get used to this.

When the lift stops we get out and go into his apartment. He is still holding my hand and he opens the balcony door, he takes me out by the hand and makes me stand up against the balcony. He stands behind me and wraps his arms around me. "Is this what you wanted Tasha?"

"Yeah Caleb, this feels like a small piece of heaven right here." I say leaning against his chest.

He groans into my ear and kisses my neck, "I know you've been through so much in the last couple of months Tasha, I'm here for you morning, noon and night! There is nothing I won't do for you. You don't ever need to be scared of me, I won't break your heart I promise. I also promise here and now not to push you into anything you don't want to do! I will leave the pace of our relationship up to you and will stick by your decisions. I want to make you mine in every possible way that I can, but I know that you're not ready for that." I blush because I know he means sex and I'm grateful for him not pushing me, that takes the pressure off me anyway.

I turn in his arms, "Caleb I don't know what I ever did to deserve you in my life. Thank you for understanding my fears and I know you'll help me through each and every one of them when the times comes." I wrap my arms around his neck and pull his head down so that I can kiss his lips.

"God Tasha you're kisses are my new drug of choice." he groans into my mouth. I'm not sure how long we stood on the balcony just huddled together in silence but when we move back inside I can see the time is 11 o'clock.

"Do you want me to take you home Tasha? It's getting late, I know you're worried about your parents." he says touching my cheek.

"I'd rather you stayed but I understand if you want to go home."

I push him up against the couch until he sits down and then I sit in his lap. "I'll text Mum and let her know I'm staying here tonight if that's ok with you." I say looking in his eyes.

He smiles a smile that is so wide his eyes shine. "Thank you Tasha."

I move to get off his lap and he holds me down, I stop what I'm doing and look at him. I know he's not going to hurt me but I start to panic a little. I start trying to jump back off his lap, my eyes are wide with panic. Then he lets me go. "I'm sorry Tasha I didn't want you to get off my lap. I didn't think about what I was doing." he looks so sad and sorry.

"It's fine Caleb, I just panicked a little

but I'm fine." I smile at him so he knows that I'm ok. I reach over to my bag and get my mobile out to text Mum. I get an instant reply.

"Thanks for letting me know. I hope you know what you're doing! Love you baby girl"

I tell her I love her too and then turn to face Caleb. "Can we go to bed now I've had an exhausting evening." he smiles at me and takes my hand and drags me up the stairs.

When we are in his bedroom, I start to get panicky, "I'll give you some shorts and a t-shirt to sleep in so you don't feel uncomfortable." he says rummaging around in his drawers.

I go into the bathroom and undress and put on his clothes, when I go back into the bedroom, he's already in bed and he has the covers pulled back for me to jump in. "Can I cuddle you to sleep tonight?" He says as I get in and he starts to pull me back to his chest.

"That sounds like heaven." I say snuggling back into him.

He runs his hand up and down my arm and says, "You've made me so happy tonight, I just want to go to sleep with you in my arms and wake up to your beautiful sunny face in the morning. Anything else will be a bonus later on," he kisses the top of my head, "night night my Angel."

"Night Caleb sweet dreams."

"They always are when I dream of you." I can hear he is starting to drift off. I fall asleep quickly and peacefully.

18

When I wake up, I feel someone's arms around me and a leg draped across me, it feels so natural, but I start to panic a little bit. I start to move and the arm around me tightens. "I hope you're not changing your mind Tasha, I told you the last time you stayed over that I wanted to wake up like this every morning." he pulls me closer and kisses me on the lips. "Good morning Tasha." he smiles his gorgeous smile at me.

"Morning Caleb," I say in between kisses. "I've not changed my mind, I think this is the best decision I have made in a long time." I smile at him, he pulls me closer to his body, facing him.

He runs his hand up and down my back while he talks to me, I know he is trying to put me at ease. "I have waited so long for you to come into my life, I thought I'd never meet someone who took my breath away and became my reason to breathe and then you fell into my life. I told you that it was destiny and I still believe that. Tasha, I promise you that I will protect you and love you until my dying breath. My Angel!" he kisses me so gently if I wasn't looking at him I wouldn't have felt it.

"Caleb, when I bumped into you that night, my life was so different and it changed that night, not for the best as you know, but you came into my life and you were the only one I could talk to through that hard time and I will always be grateful for that. You have come into my life and have consumed my thoughts and I know that my life will still have some obstacles but I know that you will be there helping me along. That makes my life easier to live." I kiss him, not so softly on the lips, I want my emotion to come out in the kiss.

I feel his cock in between us and I know I need to address the subject of sex and I'm embarrassed. "Can I ask you something?"

"You don't need to ask that - you can talk to me about anything Tasha." he says smiling at me.

"What if I can't, you know," I look down at the bed, "you know, can't have sex because of what happened to me. What will you do then? Will you leave me?" I can feel a tear coming out of my eye, because I don't want to lose him, I've only just found him.

He puts his finger on my chin and lifts it so I am looking in his eyes. "Hey Tasha I'm not going to give up on you that easy, I want you in my life in whatever capacity I can. I want to help you through any issues you might have. You have been through a very traumatic experience and there will be repercussions, we both know that, but I am not going to give up at the first hurdle. You need to know that I am in this for the long term Tasha, I can't live without you now that I have you." he reaches over and wipes up the tears that have run out from my eyes and then he leans in and kisses each of my eyes, "Come on Tasha."

"Caleb that is so beautiful, no one has ever said anything to me like that. I promise that if I'm worried about anything that I will talk to you about it. Now I think we need to get up before Caleb junior gets carried away." I laugh looking down under the sheet.

He laughs and it's such a beautiful sound that I want to hear it again. "Actually he doesn't feel very junior." I say.

He keeps laughing and then he says, "Maybe we should get up, I'm not sure he can restrain himself for much longer if you keep looking at him."

I roll onto my back and laugh, it feels so good to laugh.

We get up and go downstairs for coffee, I know I have to get home and make sure Mum knows I'm ok and I want to talk to her about what happened last night. I know I'm not going to be staying with them long, but I still respect my parents.

After a leisurely breakfast, we walk down town so that I can go and get my car from the office. We hold hands walking along the street and it feels so natural and it feels wonderful. I can feel the love coming off Caleb and as he puts his arm around my shoulders and brings me in for a hug, my heart starts racing. I know I'm majorly attracted to him, but I'm so scared about how the relationship will pan out and I don't want to lose him from my life.

"What are you thinking about Angel?" He says as he stands in front of me. "Don't worry about things that you think might happen. Let me try and put a smile back on your face." he says as he takes my face into his two hands and raises it to face him. He slowly lowers his face until his lips are grazing mine, "Tasha I could kiss you all day," and then he takes my lips and devours them. I can feel my heart picking up speed, I am really turned on and that frightens me. I relax into the kiss and enjoy it much more knowing we are standing in the middle of the street and things can't go too far. We finally pull apart and then he takes my hand again and we go find my car. I climb in and ask if he wants a lift, "No thanks Tasha, I'm going to go for a coffee and meet Dillon, if I can't be with you then he'll have to do." he laughs, leans into the car and kisses me like he won't see me again.

"Wow I'll say goodbye more often Caleb if it means you'll kiss me like that every time." I smile at him.

He laughs and say, "I don't want to say goodbye Tasha but I know you have things to do. Will I get to see you tonight maybe? We could go for dinner?" he looks nervous when he asks.

I reach out the window and touch his face, "I will ring you later and make arrangements to see you tonight. I think I would find it hard to go without my Caleb fix," I laugh. "I'll see you later Caleb." I smile and then drive off laughing and smiling in the mirror.

19

I've laughed more in the last 24 hours than I have in the last 2 months, I have a good feeling about Caleb but I really need to talk to Mum. I ring her from the car, "Mum I'm on my way home, can I take you out for lunch? I really need to talk to you, I need some Mummy advice."

She laughs at me, "Of course we can go out for lunch, will I invite Dad? or is it a girlie chat?"

"It's a girlie chat I need, I'll talk to Dad another time." I laugh. "I'll be there in 15 minutes so be ready and we can go to The White Lion Bar, it's my favourite place."

I hang up and think about what I need to talk to Mum about, there are a few things

I really need to talk about, I will have to stay focused. I ring Kammie while I'm driving,

"Hey bitch." she says when she answers the phone. She asks me about my first week at work and how things are with Caleb. I tell her about last night. "Way to go Tasha, he is such a nice guy, he cares about you a lot, just don't forget you've been through a lot and he's helped you, but don't mix up your feelings for him just because he helped you, if that make sense." I laugh at her because I do understand. I make arrangements to meet her on Wednesday after work.

I pull into my drive and when I get to the door Mum is ready and waiting for me, she is smiling at me, "You look well baby girl, you look happy." she takes me into her for a hug.

"Thanks Mum, now I'm going to get changed see you in 5 minutes." I smile as I pull away from her.

When I come back down Mum is waiting for me, we say goodbye to Dad and get into the car and drive off. We talk about nothing in general as I drive us to the hotel, we go into the hotel, order a drink and then sit where we can see the view out of the window. I don't really know how to start the conversation, but I just need to get so much out, "Mum I need to talk about a few things and I know I will waffle a bit but I need to get them off my chest."

"Ok Tasha," she says laughing, "you won't say anything that I can't already guess, so do your worst." she takes a sip of her drink.

I laugh because I'm nervous, "Firstly, I just wanted to say thank you for how you and Dad have been with me over the last while, I know it's been hard and I don't know what I would have done without the two of you to help to get me through what has to be the toughest time of my life, so far." I take a drink and then say, "I appreciate staying with you and Dad and I know you don't think I should sell the house, but I really can't go back there and live there with all my memories, so I've put the house on the market and I'm going to look for an apartment. Caleb has a few properties and said I could stay in one of his, so I might take him up on it."

"Ok baby girl, I knew it wouldn't be long before you moved out, I hoped you wouldn't be moving in with Kammie or Caleb for that matter, I'm glad you still want your independence."

"Yeah, I figured that I need my own space, I sometimes get anxious when I'm with Caleb on my own, not because I think he is going to hurt me, but because Felix hurt me when there was no one else around and no one would have thought that he would do that to me, the one he loved. I feel like I need to have some time on my own for a while to be able to do what I want when I want, not what Felix wanted me to do. Does that make sense?" I take another sip of my drink because I know I'm waffling.

"Sweetheart, of course it makes sense. I can see now that Felix was changing for a while, he wasn't letting you have the freedom that you should have had and he did it in a way that no one was aware of it. Just because you want to move out doesn't mean we won't see you anymore, I know for a fact you will be home for Sunday dinner." she laughs, she knows how much I love her Sunday dinners.

"Thanks for understanding Mum, I knew you would. Now, the other thing I wanted to talk to you about is Caleb." I look at Mum and I see her raise her eyebrows and roll her eyes.

"He means a lot to me Mum, I know I haven't known him long and I know he has helped me through a really bad time and that I am probably just grateful to him for doing that, but I think he really likes me and I need to seriously think about that." I take another sip and I can feel a tear in my eye, but I don't allow it to fall. I tell Mum about last night in the pub and then back at the apartment, I'm nervous telling her because she is my Mum and I'm her little girl but I need to talk about things that she needs to listen to, help me to understand and help me to get through them.

"Tasha, I know Caleb has a lot of feelings for you, I have spoken to him and I like him, I can see he cares for you a lot. I also think that you might like him as much as you do because he helped you through all of this but, you have to remember, he WAS there for you, he was the one you spoke to about all of this, he didn't run off, he didn't tell you to stop talking to him. He knew you were married and he wanted to be your friend with no ulterior motive, keep that in mind, he thinks a lot of you Tasha." she says patting my arm.

We sit in silence for a while and then I start talking again, "I know how much he cares for me Mum, I know I care for him too. He makes me feel safe and secure and I love the feeling, I crave that feeling right now. I told Caleb that I would be his girlfriend and I really want to be with him and give it a go. I know I've been through hell, but I just want to forget it, as much as I can and get on with my life. I deserve a bit of happiness and I'm going to take it where I can."

"Here, here baby girl." Mum raises her glass to mine. I laugh and follow suit.

"So, the last thing I wanted to talk to you about I think I need another drink for," I stand up and go and order a drink for us both. When I sit back down I say, "I want to talk to you about sex." I see Mum's eyebrows lift up and then she smiles, as if she knew this was the real direction my conversation was going to take.

"Me and Caleb talked about sex last night, well, he did really because I was so embarrassed. He said that I was to set the pace of our relationship and if I didn't want to do anything sexual then he was fine with that. I don't know how, as a man, he can say that and mean it but I really believe him Mum." Our drinks arrive and this gives me a moment to breathe before carrying on. "I'm really attracted to him, Mum, he makes me feel like a beautiful woman and I know that I will want to take our relationship further, but I'm not sure if I can, you know." I blush, it is quite embarrassing talking to Mum about it maybe I should have kept this conversation for Kammie.

"Tasha, you've been through some things that no one should ever have to go through, EVER! You had an operation to repair some of the damage that Felix did to you. That doesn't mean you should stay celibate for the rest of your life. Yes I think it is too soon, but I'm not you and only you will know whether it is too soon or not, emotionally and physically. I think you will have a lot of flashbacks and it won't be easy, but I also know that Caleb will only make love to you when you are ready and he won't force you because he knows what you have been through. We can find a counsellor who specialises in this type of thing if you want baby girl. I think you've done so well by yourself, talking to me about it and I know you will talk Kammie about it too, just make sure if you want a serious relationship with Caleb that you talk to him as well. Ok honey?"

I can feel the tears finally falling down my face and I feel Mum move closer to me and hug me, "Baby girl, I love you so much and I worry about you all the time, that will never change, I also know how strong you are, how beautiful you are inside and out and how much you fight for what you want, regardless of what you have to go through to get it. Caleb is a good man and I, for one, am happy that he is looking after you, it makes me feel safe." she kisses me on the side of my head and moves back to her seat.

"Thanks Mum, I know there are a lot of situations facing me that will be hard for me, but knowing that you will be there for me will help me so much. I hope I didn't embarrass you Mum!" I say looking down at my drink, I think I am more embarrassed than she is.

"Baby girl, you can't embarrass me, I'm your Mum yes, but I hope I'm a friend too. If you need to talk about anything then I'm here for you ok?"

"Thanks Mum, I feel so much better now. I know I have to have this conversation with Kammie and also with Caleb soon otherwise it will be something that will wedge between us and I don't want that. I want something good to come out of me and him."

We sit chatting for a while longer, we laugh a lot and then we decide that we have to go home to see Dad. When we are driving home Mum says, "Do you want to invite Caleb over for Sunday dinner tomorrow Tasha?"

I nearly crash the car, I gasp and say "I'd love that Mum. Are you sure Dad won't mind, I know you'll tell him what we talked about and I don't want it to be awkward."

"Tasha, if I thought it would be awkward I wouldn't have said anything, anyway we want to get to know him if you are going to be together."

I told her I would ask him and let her know later. When we get home, I ring Caleb to find out how his coffee went with Dillon.

"It was good, we talked about last night and what happened after we left, he said everyone had a few drinks and only talked about us for about 20 minutes," he laughs. "How was your day Tasha?"

"I had a good day, I went to the White Lion Bar for a coffee with Mum, I felt like I needed to talk to her about a few things. I feel better for having had the chat," I clear my throat. "Erm Mum asked if you wanted to come to Sunday dinner tomorrow?"

"I'd love to Tasha, you must have told

her nice things about me if she wants me to come to dinner. I'm glad you spoke to someone, you know I'm here when you want to talk about anything."

"I know Caleb, thanks. Now I missed you this afternoon, can I see you tonight?"

He chuckles, "I don't think you missed me as much as I missed you and yes you will be seeing me tonight. I'll collect you at 7pm and I'll come to the door because I want to thank your parents for their dinner invite tomorrow. Do you mind if we come out to my beach house, there's something I want to show you?"

"That would be lovely Caleb, will I plan for staying over?" I ask, embarrassed.

He laughs, "Of course you can stay over, I didn't want to push you but hell yeah." I can feel him smiling.

"Great, well then I have to go and get ready for my hot date." I laugh and he does too.

"See you at 7."

"You definitely will Angel." he says goodbye then he hangs up.

I go downstairs and tell Mum and Dad that Caleb will be coming to dinner tomorrow and that I will be going out with him tonight and staying over. I don't feel embarrassed because I know I'm not ready for sex and I know Mum will tell Dad about our chat.

I go back upstairs and run the bath, I want to just sink into the hot water and think about my relationship with Caleb. I climb into the bath and sink under the water. When I come back up I lay there thinking about Felix and how he changed so much and how much I hated him for doing what he did. Then I started thinking about Caleb and how he makes me feel. While I'm thinking about him, my hands slip under the water and start running over my breasts, and down my stomach to my pussy. I gasp because I have not been touched there since Felix attacked me, I thought it would hurt, but it doesn't it feels great. I rub my fingers along my clit and then push one finger inside to see does that hurt, it doesn't so I use my other hand on my clit while plunging my finger in and out. A lot quicker than I expected I can feel the pressure building, I don't slow down because I really need to find the release. When I cum it makes me cry out because it feels so good. Maybe sex won't be so difficult after all.

I wash my hair while I'm in the bath and then when I step out I cover my body in oil to moisten my skin. I can see my cheeks have a bit of colour in them from my orgasm, it suits me. I start laughing because I started thinking that I need at least one orgasm a day to start to look healthy, I found this thought amusing.

20

Once I'm dressed I head down stairs and have a glass of wine with Mum and Dad, they tell me I look nice. Just then the doorbell rings and Mum answers the door, it's Caleb and she asks him in. He shakes her hand and says, "Thank you for the dinner invite tomorrow, I'd love to come along."

"You don't have to shake my hand just give me a hug," she says as she draws him into a hug. She whispers in his ear, but I can hear her, "I hope you will save my baby girl and not hurt her more."

I hear him answer, "I will do my best to make her happy and I'm in this for the long haul Jean."

I'm so embarrassed but I try not to let them know I heard them. Dad stands up and goes over to shake Caleb's hand, he's a little more dubious but I'm sure Mum will put him straight when we've gone.

"So I hear you have a house on the beach and you're going there tonight, well I hope you have a good time and we can all catch up tomorrow at dinner." Dad says while shaking his hand.

I'm mortified so I say, "Ok that's all the introductions needed, come on Caleb let's go." they all laugh at me and Caleb picks up my bag by the door.

"See you tomorrow for dinner," and we walk out the door. Caleb opens the passenger door for me and helps me in, then he puts my bag in the boot and then gets in the driver's side. The car journey is quiet, but it's not uncomfortable, I can't see much out of the window because it's getting dark. "Caleb how long have you had your house on the beach? You don't mind me asking do you?"

He reaches across and takes my hand and lifts it to his mouth and kisses it gently. "Of course I don't mind Angel. I've had it for about 5 years and I love it. It was an instantaneous match, I walked in and just knew this was going to be my home. I bought it because I want to get married and have a family and this seemed like the ideal place to do that. I want my children to wake up to this every day and see how beautiful it all is."

Wow I wasn't expecting that answer.

"Did you have someone for that role when you bought the house? Or are you still looking?" I was blushing because I didn't want him to think that I would love to be in that position, I didn't want to force myself on him.

"No I didn't have anyone in mind when I bought the house and there has never been anyone who I've felt close enough to to even bring them out to see the house, until I met you Tasha. I want you to fall in love with the house, then you might fall in love with me." he looks at me when he says this and smiles.

I smile back at him, I don't really know what to say, "Well I already love the house, so let's just say I'm working on you." I take his hand to my lips and kiss his hand.

"That makes me very happy Angel, now I'm cooking dinner tonight, will you watch me and talk to me please." he asks.

"Of course I will, I like watching you in the kitchen Caleb."

The rest of the journey is spent in silence and when we arrive at the house, I gasp because I forgot how beautiful it was. "Caleb you are so lucky to have a house like this, this is only a dream to me. Thank you for letting me feel welcome here."

"You are welcome anywhere I go Tasha,

anywhere." he smiles and gets out of the car and comes round to my side to open the door for me. When he helps me out of the car, he doesn't move away from me, he pushes me against the car and kisses me like his life depends on it to breathe, "I wanted to do that at your house, but knew I had to wait. I could kiss you all day and I wouldn't get bored, you are so beautiful Tasha." He takes my hand and pulls me into the house. "Come on lets go make some dinner." He says smiling.

We go into the kitchen and I jump up on the stool by the work surface, I can see he's been home this afternoon because the fire was on in the lounge when we passed through and there were dishes with food already prepared and cut up ready to cook. "I see you've been busy today Caleb." I say looking around me.

He smiles, "Yeah I hoped I was going to see you tonight so I bought some food and drink. I was surprised, but delighted when you asked to stay. I didn't think you would, to me it means that you trust me and that makes me so happy," all the time he is talking he is preparing and cooking the food. "I hope you're hungry Tasha"

"I am Caleb, and I wanted to stay with you, we have a few things to talk about if we are going to make a go of our relationship. I know that sounds serious and so soon into our relationship but I feel like we need to be honest and open with each other. I've been through too much from not being honest and I want our relationship to work." I know I'm waffling but I need him to understand.

"I promise I will always be open with you Tasha, I don't intend to piss you off, but if I do then I hope you will tell me so that we can talk it through." He walks over and kisses me on the forehead. He walks over to the fridge and opens it, "Is white wine ok?" I say yes and watch him open a bottle and pour two glasses. I can see his muscles in his forearms flex as he pulls the cork out. He hands me my glass and gives me a quick kiss on the lips. "Dinner will be about half an hour so will we sit in the lounge by the fire and talk?" he asks as he holds out his hand for me to take and follow him. I do as he wants.

"Come on then let's see how nice this fire is." I say following behind him. When we get into the lounge there is low music playing and we sit in front of the fire, with him leaning up against the sofa and I sit in between his legs leaning back onto his chest. It feels very familiar and very comfortable. It feels like this is where I belong.

"It is where you belong Angel," he chuckles.

"Oh crap did I just say that out loud?" I laugh too because I'm embarrassed.

"You did and I'm delighted you think

that." He pulls me closer and kisses me on the top of my head and wraps one arm around me. "I'd love to sit like this all night Tasha, just having you here in my house, sitting with me like this is a dream come true for me. I'm so glad you came into my life, it has been so much better since you did." I lean into him and we both sit there looking at the fire in complete silence, a comfortable silence.

After about 10 minutes of silence, Caleb says, "I don't want to move you because I like sitting here with you like this, but dinner is ready and I don't want to serve you up burnt dinner Tasha." he slowly moves me so that he can stand up and then pulls me up his body and gives me a steamy kiss. I take his hand and we go into the kitchen and I help to bring the dishes to the dining table. This is a stunning area overlooking the decking and the sea. It's beautiful, I could sit and look at this view all night, it's so peaceful.

We enjoy a lovely dinner and talk about ourselves, we get to know each other better. We laugh and ask questions about our lives before meeting. I don't talk about Felix and Caleb doesn't ask.

After we have finished dinner and cleared away the dishes we go back into the lounge and sit in front of the fire again, although this time Caleb sits on the sofa and pulls me down to sit on his lap. This is comfortable too, however, I start to panic a little because I can feel the mood changing and Celeb is kissing me deeper and more urgently now.

"Caleb as much as I enjoy what you're doing right now, I think we need to talk about sex." I say looking at the floor.

"Ok if that's what you want, we don't need to yet Angel I can control myself, honestly." he says putting his finger under my chin and lifting it up so he can kiss me.

"I know you can Caleb, but I'd like to talk about it so it doesn't become the white elephant in the room, is that ok?"

He nods and takes hold of my hand, "You start Tasha and you decide on the pace."

"Ok, I'm embarrassed but I need to get this off my chest, I am really attracted to you physically Caleb and I want to take our relationship to the next stage but I'm worried how I'll react after the last time I was intimate. I think to do that I need to tell you what happened between me and Felix, you need to understand why I might react in a certain way. Is that ok? Do you mind me telling you?"

I turn to face him because I'm scared he's going to say no! This is too much for anyone to deal with, I start to move off his lap to stand up. He reaches out and grabs my hand, "Sit down Tasha, I'm not hesitating because I don't want to hear it or because I can't cope with what you're going to say, I'm hesitating because I don't want you to have to go through it all again, I don't want to see you suffer. If you want to tell me, then I'll listen but I can't promise that I won't get angry - not at you but at Him!" he pulls me back onto his lap and wraps his arms around me.

"I need to do this Caleb or I won't be able to move on. It all started on our wedding day or at least that's when I realised something was different." I sit on his lap and tell him the whole story including Felix pushing me down the stairs, the night of the ball and how he assaulted me and the last night, the night I got the job offers and went through the contracts and what happened in the bedroom that night. I had tears running down my face, I couldn't help it, I can't believe I went through all of that.

"Can I touch you Angel, I want to comfort you, but I don't want to upset you." he says as he reaches out to touch my face. I nod my head and he slowly touches my cheeks, "Tasha I can't believe that anyone could put you through all of that. I won't push you into anything, honestly. I just want to protect you and look after you."

I look up at him and I can see he has tears in his eyes, "Caleb, don't get upset, it happened and I've moved on, I need to forget it so that I can have a proper relationship with you, I have so many feelings for you and it scares me because I don't want to disappoint you Caleb, I'm falling hard for you." I look up into his eyes and see the surprise there. "I want everything with you." I move so that I'm straddling him and facing him, I lean into him and kiss him on the lips. "I want to be worth it for you Caleb." I kiss him again and force my tongue into his mouth, he kisses me back, the kiss is so full of emotions from both of us.

"Tasha you are so amazing, to be able to go through all of that and come out the other side and be such a wonderful person. I promise you I won't ask you to do anything you don't want to do ok Angel, I promise." We sit on the couch with me facing him and him holding me to his chest for quite a while.

"Tasha will you take a walk with me on the beach, I feel like some fresh air." I lean back and tell him that I would, so I get off him and then he takes my hands, stands up, we grab our coats and walk out onto the decking.

"Caleb this is so beautiful, I can't believe you actually live here."

"Not as often as I would like Tasha, but if I had someone to share it with someday then I'd gladly drive to work every day from here" he pulls me in close and puts his shoulder around me. "I wanted to show you how it looked at night! It's really special at night!"

We walk along the beach for about half an hour, "It's getting cold we need to go back home, I want to get you in bed so I can snuggle up to you all night."

I didn't think about staying over and sleeping in a bed next to him, I'm sure I can do this, but I find him so attractive, maybe we can try something and see how we go.

"Come on then Caleb let's go back, let's go to bed." I say.

"I've been waiting a long time to hear you say that Angel." he laughs. We go back to the house and then Caleb locks the house down and we go up to his room. It really is huge, and beautiful but so masculine.

I start to get my things out of my bag and I can feel Caleb looking at me, "Is everything ok Caleb?" I ask as I turn to find him staring at me with his mouth open.

"Tasha you are so beautiful I'm so lucky you fell into my life." he walks towards me and kisses me so tenderly on the mouth. He stands back and starts to take off his clothes but leaves his boxers on, although they don't leave anything to the imagination as they are tight fitting to his gorgeous body. I know I'm staring as I gulp a breath I look up and see him watching me with laughter in his eyes. I can feel a blush coming over my face and he smiles.

"Are you wearing just that in bed?" I ask.

"Does it make you uncomfortable Tasha?" he asks smiling.

"Not really just preparing myself, back in a minute." I turn and walk into the bathroom. When I walk out he is already in bed waiting for me, I climb in beside him and he pulls me to him. I'm facing him and he pushes me slowly onto my back and while he kisses me, his hands start to rub up and down my body, feeling their way around. When his hand moves between my legs I start panicking, I jump back and jump off the bed. I start screaming and sit in the corner of the room just rocking back and forth.

I don't know how long I'm like that but my throat feels hoarse and my clothes are wet. Caleb is sat in front of me as white as a ghost. "Tasha tell me you're ok, I want to comfort you but I don't want to scare you." I slowly look up at him to see he has tears on his face too, he knows I've seen them. "Tasha I'm so worried that you'll hate me for touching you like that, I'm sorry, I wasn't going to go any further I promise. I would never do anything to hurt you. I promise." I know he is telling the truth.

"Hold me Caleb, please." I say and he takes me and lifts me onto his lap and he rests against the wall as he wraps his arms around me and makes me feel comfortable again. I must have fallen asleep on his lap because when I open my eyes I am in the bed and it is morning time.

21

I start moving to turn and look at Caleb when he says, "Good Morning Tasha, come here," and he pulls me closer to him. I feel safe when I am this close to him. He makes me feel safe.

After breakfast we drive to Mum and Dad's for dinner, it was strange just the four of us, but they made Caleb feel really welcome and I can't thank them enough for that.

Before I know it it's Wednesday and I'm meeting Kammie in our favourite pub after work. She's already there when I come in and waves me over. She has already ordered a cocktail and I smile at her. We haven't done this for so long I give her a big hug and tell her I love her.

She smiles and says, "love you too bitch." and then she laughs.

We sit and pass the time with general chit chat, my health, my job, her job and then we talk about Luca.

"How are things going with Luca Kammie?" I ask because I want all the juicy details.

She smiles and says, "Great absolutely great, I can't believe there was a time when he wasn't there for me. He stays at my place most nights and I love it!"

"That's great Kammie you deserve to be happy."

"So Tasha tell me about Caleb, what's going on with you two?"

I signal for the waiter to bring us more cocktails and then I say, "Everything is going so well, he makes me feel like the most beautiful person on earth, he is always doing things for me, it feels like we are two parts molded together, I never thought it would feel this good, what I had with Felix was nowhere near as intense as my feelings for Caleb. Does that mean that I didn't really love Felix? Then again I had agreed to spend the rest of my life with him so I know I loved him. I think I'm just confused that's all."

The waiter puts our drinks down and we lift them in the air for a toast, "Here's to new love." Kammie says.

We both take a sip of our drinks and then I carry on, "Kammie I need to talk to you about something, I'm a little bit embarrassed and don't know what to do."

She leans in towards me, "Sounds intriguing carry on."

I take a deep breath, "I want to talk about sex." I look around me because I'm getting embarrassed. "I don't know if I can have sex with Caleb, Kammie." I can feel the tears welling up, "we talked about it and he's happy for me to lead the way, which I'm not used to doing. I really fancy him and love when his body is touching mine, but I'm so scared."

"Tell me exactly what you're scared of Tasha," she says taking my hand and rubbing it.

"I'm scared he won't stick around and help me get past the barriers I've got about sex, what if he gets bored of waiting Kammie? I don't know what I'd do. We were in bed the other night and we were cuddling and he was rubbing his hand up and down my body, when we started getting more intimate, I screamed and dived out of the bed and went to the corner of the room, slid down the wall onto my honkers and just rocked back and forth. It was so embarrassing!"

"Oh god Tasha, I didn't think about how you would cope with being intimate again.

I'm sorry for everything that has happened to you and I will do whatever I can to help you move on from Felix. Tell me what did Caleb do when you went into the corner?" she asked.

I wipe my eyes and try to talk, but it's hard so I take another few sips of my drink. I've had quite a few already and I know I won't be able to drive home. "He flew out of the bed, came over to the corner, he sat in front of me and asked could he hug me, when I said yes he moved behind me, put me onto his lap and held me, he rocked me to and fro and we sat like that for about half an hour, I must have fallen asleep. Then he lifted me into his arms and took me to bed and cuddled me all night. I felt really bad though, he doesn't need to put up with that, there must be other women out there who can make him happy and have sex with him Kammie, it's just not fair."

"Tasha from what I know about Caleb, something like that isn't going to stop him from getting what he wants and he wants you. He will wait until you're ready, he is in this for the long term he told Luca that you know. I think he's fallen in love with you, he can't take his eyes off you whenever you are in the room. You deserve his love and don't you dare think anything else."

"Thanks Kammie, but I'm sure he would be happier without me around to make his life miserable. My body wants him, but somehow I can't get passed what happened. I told him all about Felix and what happened since I met him in the nightclub, I felt that he needed to know so that he could understand any issues that I had. However, I don't think it's fair to him." I am crying again because the thought of giving Caleb up makes me so upset.

"Tasha don't be silly you can't just give up on someone like Caleb, he won't let you for one and you both have something so special that only comes along once in your life, you need to keep him Tasha, you know that though. Don't give up at the first hurdle Tasha, he's worth more than that."

We sit quietly for a few minutes then Kammie says to me, "Tasha, I know you don't want to talk about this but just in case you forgot. Luca reminded me last night that he still has Felix's suicide note that he left for you. Do you think if you read it you might feel better?"

"Oh god Kammie, I forgot all about that. I don't want to read it, it'll bring it all up again and I don't think I can deal with that." I say while swirling my drink around in my glass.

"Look Luca just text me and he's around the corner with Caleb, they met up because Caleb was worried about you after the other night, do you mind them coming in here. I think Caleb needs to see how worried you are and maybe we can all talk about things to try and help you." she says sheepishly. "If you don't want them to come here then that's fine, but Luca really needs to talk to you about this Tasha."

I think about this for a while and then say, "I don't mind Kammie, it might help." and I sit back in my chair drinking more of my cocktail while she texts Luca to let him know that they should both come into the pub.

It takes them about 10 minutes and me and Kammie don't talk, we just stare into our drinks.

"Hey girls," Luca says coming over to us, he leans over and kisses me on the forehead and then kisses Kammie on the mouth and sits next to her.

"Hey," Caleb says nodding to Kammie and coming over to me and kissing me on the lips and then sitting next to me and takes my hand.

"Hey guys," Kammie says, "Can't last a night out without us huh?" she says laughing.

"No we can't, we missed you terribly." Caleb says laughing, his thumb is rubbing my hand, to make sure I am ok.

I smile up at him and lean across and kiss him on the lips. "It's good to see you guys, glad you decided to come and join us."

We sit and talk for a while and then I say, "Luca I understand you have something you want to give me."

He finishes taking a sip of his drink, which has arrived while we were all chatting. "Yeah am I ok to talk about it with you Tasha?" I nod my head and so he continues, "That afternoon that I came to the house when you rang me, I found a note in the bedroom, leaning up on your bedside table. It had your name on it so I took it, I didn't think you wanted the police to find it and read it. I still have it Tasha and I think you should read it, I know he was a sadistic bastard at the end, but he loved you and I don't think you can move on without reading it Tasha." he looks up at me and sees that I have a couple of tears running down my face.

Caleb turns to face me, "Tasha I think Luca is right, I think you need to read the note for some sort of closure. You need to realise that whatever Felix did to you it was nothing to do with anything that you did, it was all him and his state of mind. Maybe you can move on if you read the letter. We can all be there when you read it or you can read it on your own, it's your choice Angel."

I take a few deep breaths and look at the three expectant faces, "I think I'd rather read it alone if you don't mind, Luca I'll get the letter off you at the weekend if that's ok?"

"Yeah that's fine Tasha as long as you're sure you want to do this on your own." Luca says.

I nod my head, "yes I am."

We all sit there in silence for a while and then the waiter comes over and asks do we want another drink, we all order another one and then we start chatting again. I know I've had too many to drink and I start slurring and start to get dizzy.

"Come on Tasha I think it's time for you to go home." Caleb says and helps me up from the chair. "You can stay at my place again tonight. Guys if you want to stay too you can, it's easier than finding a cab to take you all the way home."

They both agree and we start to leave the pub, when I hit the fresh air I start to giggle because I really am drunk. I stagger for a while and then I feel light as a feather, I realise that Caleb is carrying me. I look up into his face, "I love you Caleb." I say and then start giggling.

He stops and stands still. "Angel I've been waiting for you to say that to me, it makes me feel so amazing that someone as beautiful as you could love someone like me. I'm going to wait until you're sober to tell you exactly how I feel about you." I smile up at him.

We all go back to Caleb's place and he walks upstairs and undresses me for bed, he gently places me into the bed, pulls the duvet up and kisses me on the head. "I'll be back in a little while Tasha, I need to make sure your friends are ok."

I hold his hand and smile at him and then pull him back down to kiss me, "Thanks Caleb." I can feel my eyes getting heavy.

I toss and turn quite a bit even though I am tired, my mind is wondering to Felix and everything that has happened, I think it's because we were talking about it this evening and it brought a lot back. I try to go to sleep and then sometime during the night I feel myself being pulled across the bed, I don't panic though because I can smell Caleb. When he wraps his body around mine I moan in my sleep. He chuckles. "I am madly in love with you Tasha and I can't wait to tell you when the time is right. I will wait until you are ready so that I can take all of you as mine." he pulls me closer and kisses me on my shoulder. I fall straight to sleep and have a peaceful night's sleep.

22

When I wake up the next morning, my head is pounding and I feel Caleb behind me in the bed, I start to move away from him, when I feel his hand reach over to my stomach and start to pull me backwards, he moans. I think he is still asleep, I giggle because even in his sleep he wants me.

"Are you laughing at me Tasha?" he says not letting me go.

"Yes I am Caleb, you were moaning in your sleep and pulling me back into you."

"I didn't want you to get up and leave me." he says kissing my shoulder.

All of a sudden I see the sun shining through the window. "Caleb what time is it? What time is it?" I start to panic, its

Thursday morning and I'm leisurely lying in bed.

He slowly turns around in the bed and says, "Its 10.30 Tasha."

I sit upright in the bed. "Caleb it's Thursday and I should've been in work two hours ago." I'm starting to panic, I jump out of bed, "Fuck, fuck, fuck." I turn around and he is still in bed and he's laughing.

"Caleb it's not funny get out of bed." I'm yelling now.

"Tasha you look so funny running around not really achieving anything, slow down, calm down, sit down on the bed it's alright I sorted it." He starts patting the bed for me to sit down. I go over and sit down where he says.

"Caleb I hope you didn't ring in sick for me, I don't want any special favours because I'm your girlfriend. You know how I feel about that." I stop shouting to take a big breath. He reaches out and touches me on the arm, I take another breath and turn to look at him.

"Tasha I rang earlier and told them I have a meeting to attend and I wanted you to come with me because it's a new project we are working on together. Don't worry you'll be going into work after lunch, I know you need recognition for your work and I wouldn't do anything to change that. Now come here and give me a good morning kiss, please." he grabs me by the hand and pulls me on top of him and I kiss him with raw emotion because I knew he wouldn't really have rang in sick for me he knows how I feel about that. His hands start to rundown my back and I can feel a warm fuzzy feeling building, maybe I can do this.

I can hear myself moaning into his mouth because his hands feel so good, he rolls me over on the bed and props himself up on one elbow, "Tasha can I kiss you all over, I don't want anything else from you but I want to show you how much you mean to me?"

I nod because I can't speak, I'm so full of emotions right now, he is such a wonderful person. I let him kiss me again on the lips then he leans up and kisses me on my eyes, then my cheeks, then my neck, my collar bone, then small kisses all the way down to my breasts. He looks up at me and I can see the question in his eyes, I nod again and he continues down to my nipple, he kisses it so softly I nearly didn't feel it, he then moves over to the other one and does the same. He looks up at me again with another question is his eyes, I nod again and take a deep breath. He slowly licks my nipple and then takes it fully into his mouth and sucks very gently on it, I feel my back arch to get closer to his mouth and I hear myself moan.

He looks at me and then moves back

over to the first nipple, he licks in then takes it fully into his mouth and sucks on it gently I arch my back again, he looks up at me and then when I nod my head he continues down my body, slow small kisses down my stomach to my belly button, he takes my belly bar into his mouth and then smiles up at me. He looks for confirmation once again to keep going, I gulp then nod my head, I need to try to make this work. He keeps kissing me down from my belly button until he reaches the top of my panties, he kisses them and moves past them.

What!?!? I was preparing myself for him kissing me there, when he looks up at me this time he has mischief in his eyes, I lay back on the bed and laugh. "You're a tease Caleb," he chuckles and I can feel the vibration at the top of my leg where he has his mouth, he kisses slowly down the inside of one leg and then my ankle and then he slowly kisses back up the other leg. When he reached my panties he looks at me again, I can feel myself panting and I nod my head and throw it back on the bed, I can feel myself start to stiffen up as he kisses me on top of my panties from the top of them down to my lips. The sensation is amazing and I'm sure my panties are wet right now, he looks at me again and when I nod my head he starts to gently pull my panties down. When he has them down enough he kisses my bare skin all the way down to my lips.

I hear him groan and then, with his mouth still on me, he says, "God Angel you're wet and you smell gorgeous, I can't wait to taste you, but I promised I would only kiss you and that's what I'm going to do," he pulls my panties up and continues to kiss me until he reaches my nipples and he takes one into his mouth and flicks it with his tongue, I can't believe I can feel the pressure rising in my body and I want to close my legs to make it go away, but I can't because he's lying between them. "Just let it go Tasha, please," he takes the other nipple and does the same, flicking with his tongue then sucking it and I'm all done and can't take it anymore. I fall over the edge and have the most amazing orgasm I've ever had. I don't think I've had an orgasm from someone kissing me before. I shout "C A L E B" as the waves take over my body.

"Oh my god that was beautiful, you are beautiful" he comes up and takes my mouth in his and I can feel the hunger in his kiss, I can feel his arousal against my body, I reach down to take his cock in my hand and he moves so that I can't reach it.

"Caleb please I need to look after you too, that was amazing." he takes my hand and laces our fingers together.

"Tasha that was all about you, baby steps that's what I want to take, we have the rest of our life for everything else, but now we just take things one stage at a time ok." I can feel the tears running down my face, he leans over and kisses them off me. "Come on Angel," and he hugs me and pulls me onto my side so we are facing each other. "Do you remember what you said to me last night Tasha?" he searches my face for an answer.

I try to rack my brains to see if I can remember and then it hits me when he carried me in town I told him I loved him. I blush and can't look at him, "Yes I do."

"Did you mean it Tasha? Or was it just because you were drunk?" he asks.

"I I I meant it but I don't think I should have said it yet, we're still very new in our relationship and I don't want to frighten you off Caleb."

"You don't frighten me Tasha, what we have together should frighten both of us, but I think that we were born to love each other and help each other and to be together. You hold that thought and you'll tell me again when you're ready. Now let's get up and get ready, we have a meeting to attend." he says winking at me.

23

After work on Friday I've arranged for Caleb to come over for about 7.30pm and Luca around the same time. I get changed and go down to wait for them to come over. Mum has been cooking all afternoon and the smell is delicious. Caleb is first to arrive and brings flowers for Mum, Luca arrives about 10 minutes later and gives Mum a kiss. We all sit down to dinner and talk about nothing real important, then when dinner is finished we move into the lounge and have more wine. Luca starts the conversation that I have been dreading all night, "Tasha I know you don't really want to talk about this, but I need to pass this letter over to you, Felix meant for you to read it and I think it will help you to move forward in your life." He reaches into his back pocket and hands me an envelope which has "*Natasha*" written on in his handwriting, seeing that makes me feel sad. I take the letter and inadvertently smell it, I do that sometimes with things.

I put it into my back pocket of my jeans and steer the conversation to something else, although I can see everyone looking at me and waiting for me to say or do something. I ignore them and just carry on the evening as if I didn't just get the letter.

A couple of hours later, Luca stands up and says that he is leaving, Caleb stands up too. "Tasha I'm going to leave with Luca and we can share a cab home, will I see you tomorrow?"

He seems worried, I walk over to him and whisper in his ear, "I wish you didn't have to go, I love sleeping with you next to me."

I pull back and see him smile at me, "me too." he says.

I walk them both to the door after they have said goodbye to Mum and Dad. Luca walks out to the cab and Caleb turns to face me, "Goodnight my Angel." And kisses me forcefully on the mouth, I feel his tongue sliding into my mouth and I reach up and pull his head closer to mine, he puts his arms around me and pulls me into a hug. "God Tasha I don't want to leave you here, come home with me?"

I pull away slightly, "I can't Caleb, I need to talk to Mum and Dad about the letter and decide what I'm going to do, I'll call you in the morning ok."

He nods his head and then kisses me once more. "See you tomorrow Tasha," and then he walks over to the cab and leaves with Luca.

I wait until their cab is at the end of the street before I turn and go into the house. I lean my back up against the front door, take a deep breath and walk into the kitchen to see Mum and Dad cleaning up and Dad has put the coffee machine on. "Oh Dad that is just what I want right now, a cup of coffee," I walk over and give him a kiss and then help Mum to clean up. We all sit at the kitchen table and drink our coffee, I will never sleep tonight now!

"So, baby girl what are you going to do with that letter burning a hole in your pocket?" Mum says, always one not to hold back.

"I'm going to read it tomorrow I think, but I want to be on my own to read it, is that ok?" I ask.

"Of course it is, if you need me to be there then I will be ok," she leans over and kisses me on the head.

When I've finished my coffee I stand and tell them I'm going to bed and I go up the stairs.

After I've got undressed, I climb into bed and check my phone and there is a message from Caleb.

"Hey Tasha thanks for a lovely night, your Mum cooks nice food. I wish you would have come home with me tonight but I understand why you didn't. Hopefully I'll see you tomorrow, miss you already xxx"

"Night Caleb, thanks for coming over, I know you'll be there for me when I need you, you always are. Thanks for helping me through the hard times. Xxx"

I turn my phone off and close my eyes, I'm soon asleep.

I start dreaming about Felix and how perfect my life was until I got married, I dream about everything that has happened to me since that beautiful day. I start to panic in my dream as Felix gets worse and worse and then when he starts to attack me for the last time I start to scream and cry at the same time.

"Tasha, baby girl come on its ok I'm here, it's Mum,"

I can hear Mum's voice but I can't see her, I'm confused. "Mum, Mum, help me please." I scream.

"Baby girl, I'm here with you, open your

eyes, it's a dream, come on open your eyes," she says while rubbing my arm.

I slowly open my eyes and she leans forward and takes me into a hug. "Come on baby girl, you've been so strong, please." she's sobbing.

"Mum it hurts so much." I can feel myself getting hysterical, "Mum it hurts so much, I can't breathe, I can't breathe."

Next I hear Dad come into the room. "Move over Jean let me in there," he says and he takes me into a hug. "Come on baby girl it's ok, we're here for you, we will protect you." he says.

"Daddy I can't breathe, it hurts so much," I know I'm a bit delirious, but I can't seem to calm down, "I need Caleb Daddy, I need him, please, he can calm me down."

Mum turns my phone on and I can hear her on the phone, "Caleb it's Jean, can you come straight over, I know it's the middle of the night, Tasha needs you, she's asking for you, we can't calm her down, please hurry. Ok, yes, see you in a few minutes."

"Baby girl he's on his way, try to calm down, can I give you anything?" Mum says, I can tell she's upset.

"Mum it hurts so much, what did I do to deserve this, what!?!" I know I'm shouting but I can't help it. I rant on and on for about 15 minutes when Mum disappears and then I hear the heavy steps on the stairs and I can feel Caleb come into the room.

"Angel come here, I'll help you." Caleb says as he walks over and takes me off my Dad. He pulls me to the floor so that he can lean against the bed and then he starts rocking, just like he did in his room the other night.

"Caleb I can't breathe, it hurts so much." I cry.

"I know Tasha, I know. You are so brave, so strong you can get through this, I'm here Angel and I'm not going anywhere I promise." he's still rocking me back and forth.

I can hear my Mum crying and my Dad comforting her, I can feel myself start to calm down. I snuggle into Caleb and start breathing normally. I don't know how long I've been sitting on his lap, but I can feel my eyes getting heavy.

I hear Caleb say to Mum, "Jean is it ok if I put her in bed and climb in with her? Do you mind? I don't want to upset you."

"Caleb of course it's ok, she needs you I understand that, please do whatever you need to do to calm her down and make her feel safe. Thanks for coming back to help her, it means so much to me and us," she says coming over and kissing me on the cheek and then kissing Caleb on the head. Dad comes over and says, "Caleb I would shake your hand right now but you have your hands full, thank you for taking care of our daughter." he rests his hand on Caleb's shoulder while he says this.

"It's nothing I'll look after her for as long as she wants me to, I love her and she is my forever." he says kissing me on the head. I hear Mum and Dad leave the room and then Caleb says to me. "Now Angel I need to move you to the bed and then I'm going to get in beside you and hold you all night so you don't have any more nightmares." he slowly slides me off his lap and then lifts me into the bed, he doesn't even undress himself but just climbs in behind me. "I mean it Tasha, I love you and I want to be here for you whenever you need me." he kisses me on the shoulder and wraps his arm around me and pulls me close. "Forever Angel, Forever."

"Thanks for coming to help me Caleb, I love you too." I have a lone tear that falls from my eye, but it's a happy tear.

I fall asleep with Caleb wrapped around me and I sleep peacefully.

24

When I wake in the morning, I feel something heavy lying on top of me. I start to panic until everything that happened last night comes back to me and I realise it's Caleb. I move and he pulls me tight. "Where do you think you're going Tasha?" He kisses me on the shoulder, "Did you sleep well in the end?"

"Mmm yes I did Caleb, thanks for coming to help me, it means a lot to me." We stay wrapped up in each other for a little bit more and then I can hear Mum and Dad moving around, "Come on we better get up and go downstairs."

We get out of bed and go downstairs, Mum and Dad are both in the kitchen and look up when we come in, Mum comes over and kisses me and then moves past me and takes Caleb into a hug. "Thanks for saving my baby girl," she says to him.

When she steps back we both sit at the table and she brings coffee over for both of us.

Dad clears his throat and says to Caleb, "Thanks son for everything you have done for Tasha, you are always welcome in our house." he puts his hand on Caleb's shoulder.

Caleb says, "Thank you for letting me be a part of your daughter's life, as I said to you both last night she's my forever." he reaches across and takes my hand.

"Are you sure you're ok Tasha?" Mum says.

I nod my head. "Yes I am, I'm sorry about last night, I think everything came to a head with the letter and I started going back over everything in my dream."

We talk about nothing in particular and then Caleb says that he has to go home and change, he is off to see his parents later today. I said I would take him back to his apartment to collect his car, so when I'm changed I say goodbye to Mum and Dad and then I drive him into town to his apartment. When we arrive there, he gets out. "You know you can come with me to meet my parents Tasha, I'd love you to." he smiles.

"I know Caleb and I'd love to, but I'm not really in the right frame of mind after last night, tell them I'll meet them soon ok." he smiles at me and then leans into the window and kisses me hard.

"Take it easy today Tasha, you know where I am if you need me." I watch him walk over to the lift to go up to his apartment and when he is safely in the lift I take a deep breath and drive out of town. I stop at a coffee shop on the way and buy a latte to bring with me, I'm going to need all the strength I can get to help me through today.

I drive for about 20 minutes more and I pull into the familiar driveway. I sit in the car for a few minutes breathing heavily and trying to find the strength to do this.

I slowly step out of the car and walk up to the front door, I put the key into the lock and slowly open the door, when I walk in I close the door behind me and I lean up against it. I walk into the house where I had so many good times and as I walk through from room to room I recall the laughter and fun that we had, me and Felix. I remember him chasing me around the dining room table and me laughing so hard that he caught up with me. I remember the time when we had sex on the kitchen counter, I walk over to that counter and run my hand along the surface, taking in all the memories.

I take a sip of my coffee and then I start to walk up the stairs, I remember when Felix pushed me down the stairs and I hold on tight to the banister railing. I walk up the rest of the stairs and then slowly walk to our bedroom, my heart is racing and I start to feel palpitations, I take a few breaths and then I open the door.

As soon as I step into the bedroom, I have flashbacks of the fun we had before we got married and then the first time we came back to the house after the wedding when Felix carried me up the stairs and made love to me for hours.

I stand in the middle of the room and then look around and as I turn around the bad memories start to flood back to me, the forceful sex, the sex during the night when I was on my sleeping tablets and then the last night we had together. I back up against the wall to steady myself as I think about what happened that night. I don't want to remember, I don't want to think about it.

I slowly walk out of the bedroom and down the stairs. In the kitchen I find a lone bottle of brandy and pour some of it into my coffee. I take a big swig and then go into the lounge to sit down in the armchair.

I lean my head back on the chair and think about what I'm going to do. I reach into my back pocket and take out the letter Felix left me. I hold it in my hand and then put it on my lap. I take another drink of my coffee and then open the letter, then I take another swig and take the letter out of the envelope, then I take another swig and unfold the letter.

I put my coffee on the table and then pick the letter up in my shaking hands.

Dear Natasha

My beautiful wife. If you're reading this then I succeeded in releasing you from my clutches. I'm sorry for what I did to you and I hope you get some peace from this letter.

I've always been a possessive and jealous person way before I met you, it's always been a problem whenever I was dating. When I met you I wanted you so badly that I reined it in and managed to suppress the possessive feelings that were raging in my brain. I did really well, until the day we got married. That is when I changed, that is when we changed. That is the day the monster started to take over.

Do you remember the years, months, even

days before the wedding? We were so happy and I loved you to distraction. We had so much fun and if that could have been our forever then we would have been the most amazing family. I wanted to have your children, I wanted to be your everything.

We were good for a few years, our honeymoon was one of the best times in my life, the other was when I was standing at the altar and I turned to see you walking towards me in your beautiful dress. You were the most beautiful person in the world, but I had to go and spoil it.

When we were at work that fateful day when everything really changed and the monster within me started taking control, I tried to fight him, I really did Tasha, but he was too strong. The other guys in the office were talking about what they would love to do to you and instead of being proud that you were my wife and that they were never going to get the opportunity, the monster told me it was your fault. You had dressed provocatively for those guys in the office, I know it's not true but he was so powerful in my mind that I believed him. I tried to fight him during that first week when he appeared, but he kept taking over more and more of my mind.

I know how confused you were and how much I hurt you emotionally and physically. When we went out for Luca's birthday and I saw you talking to Mr Hunt, I saw you give him a piece of paper which I assumed was your number and the monster inside told me that you were moving on, that you didn't love me anymore. I wasn't prepared to hear any reasoning from you and I'm so sorry for what happened next.

I never wanted to hurt you and I know that I did, my apologies will never be enough for you to forgive me. What happened the last night we were together was unforgivable and I thought that I had killed you. When you passed out I started to panic, the monster had full control but there was a small part of me that knew I needed to protect you, so I moved you into the bathroom and locked the door. I did this for your safety, but I didn't know if you were alive at all. I rang Luca because I needed his help and I needed to protect you from the monster inside me. When I didn't hear you move I trashed the room and then I cut myself to stop me from hurting you. I wanted it all to be over, I wanted you to have your life, a life where you are treated the way you should be, like a princess.

When I saw you were alive I was ecstatic, but as I lay in the hospital I had so much time to think and I realised it didn't matter how much I loved you, the monster would always win. I couldn't put you through that again and I knew what I had to do.

I know you will be the first person to find me, that was not a last ditch attempt at hurting you, it was my last chance for you to see that I was setting you free, letting you live the life you deserve.

I know that you will hate me and I understand that, I even want you to hate me because I wasn't a nice person and I would have only gotten worse. Babe I love you and I did this for you.

Remember our vows Natasha? "Til Death Do Us Part"

Yours always

Felix

WOW! Where do I start, that letter just blew me away. I sit in the chair for hours just thinking of the letter, thinking about our relationship from the start through to the end. I think about our wedding day, about how my life started to change that day and then I think about the sacrifice Felix made for me to be happy.

I don't hear my phone ring, but I'm sure it must have done and I just didn't hear it because I've been gone for such a long time. I look at my phone and see I have 5 missed calls from Caleb, 4 from Mum and Dad, 4 from Kammie, 2 from Luca and loads of text messages asking where I am. I don't reply to any of them, I just need some space to think about what Felix wrote in the letter. I stand up from the armchair, walk around the house making sure everything is in order. Then I walk to the front door, turn around and face the rest of the house and say "Goodbye Felix, Goodbye Felix and Tasha, Love you, you'll always have a place in my heart." I take a deep breath and then I walk through the door for what I hope will be the last time. I lock the door and walk slowly to the car, climb in and drive away, I don't look in my rear view mirror as I leave that part of my life behind.

25

I take the scenic route home, via the Clifton Suspension Bridge, this is one of my most favourite spots. When I get home I can see Caleb's car and Luca's car outside my house, what is going on?

I park the car and run to the front door, I open it and walk in. When I get into the kitchen I freeze, everyone is staring at me. Mum, Dad, Caleb, Luca and Kammie, they are just staring and then Caleb comes over to my side so quickly I didn't even see him move! "Tasha where have you been, we've all been so worried about you, we looked for you everywhere." he pulls me into a hug.

Then Mum comes over and takes me from him. "Baby girl are you ok? You look so pale." she hugs me too.

I stand back and look around the room, there is so much love looking at me. "I'm fine guys honest, but I need a few drinks." I walk over to Dad, give him a hug then sit down at the kitchen table. Everyone follows suit and sits around the table, they are all waiting for me to speak.

Dad brings out the brandy, vodka and whiskey and places it in the middle of the table with a few mixers, then he gives everyone a glass says, "Help yourself guys I think we might need this," and he sits. Again everyone looks at me, so I speak.

"When I left Caleb back at his apartment I went over to my house to read the letter, I thought it might help. I wandered all over the house remembering my life as it was, the good memories and the bad memories together. I went into the kitchen, found some brandy, put it in my coffee that I had brought with me, then I sat in the lounge and read the letter. Luca did you read it before you gave it to me?" I ask.

He shakes his head, "No Tasha, it wasn't mine to read."

"If you don't mind I'd love to read it to you all, is that ok? I think it would help to explain Felix's actions, not that he should be forgiven, but it goes some way to explain everything."

Everyone nods their heads. "Caleb, do you mind if I read it to everyone?" I don't want him to feel uncomfortable.

"Tasha, I trust your judgment and if you feel we should all listen to it then read away, do you want me to stay or shall I go?" he is obviously uncomfortable.

"Caleb, me and you are so different from me and Felix, I want you to hear this too because this has really helped me." He nods his head at me.

I unfold the letter and take a drink of my brandy and then read the letter to them. Luca nods his head when I read the part about being a possessive and jealous boyfriend, Mum nods her head when I read about being happy before the wedding. Nobody does anything when I read the rest of the letter, when I finish I look up and I see tears in everyone's eyes, even Caleb's.

No one says anything for a few minutes, then Mum says, "That was beautiful, he knew how he was hurting you and wanted to do something about it, even if it was drastic he did the right thing for you baby girl."

Luca says, "He always was jealous and possessive, I wondered how come he wasn't with you, he was obviously trying to suppress those feelings."

Caleb says, "I can understand how he felt and why he ended it the way he did, I can totally understand his love for you Tasha, he was a good man in the end."

We all sit in silence for a while longer and I pick up my glass and hold it in the air for a toast, everyone else follows suit, "to Felix," we all clink our glasses and take a sip. We then sit at the table talking, laughing and drinking. After a while Mum gets up and orders a take away and when it comes we stay sitting at the table drinking and laughing. Before long its midnight and Luca and Kammie stand up to say they need to go, Mum says they can stay but they say no, they'd prefer to go home. Caleb stands up and says he will go with them to save getting another cab later. Mum says he can stay if he wants, he looks at me and I nod my head. "Jean if you're sure you don't mind then I would love to stay and look after Tasha." he smiles at her.

She gives him a hug, "You're always welcome."

We go to the door with Luca and Kammie to say goodbye, they both give me big hugs and Luca shakes Caleb's hand. "I'm so glad you're ok Tasha, I thought once you read the letter you would be worse because I thought he would have said something to upset you."

We wave them off and Caleb puts his arm around my shoulder and pulls me in close, "I love you Angel, you were so brave today, I'm so proud of you." he kisses me on the head and then we turn and go back to the kitchen. Mum has tidied everything away and we say goodnight and go upstairs. It feels strange to bring Caleb into my bedroom, I know he stayed the previous night, but this is different, we both undress and climb into the bed. He is wearing just his boxers and I have just my panties on.

He pulls me into his body and hugs me tight, I roll so I'm facing him and he is lying on his back, I wrap my leg over his leg and my arm across his chest. This feels like heaven. I sigh and kiss him on the chest, he pulls me closer and kisses me on the head, "You are so brave Angel, do you know that? I admire you so much."

"Thank you for understanding Caleb, I feel so much better after reading the letter. I hope it means we can move on in our relationship." I kiss him again on his chest.

He moans, "Angel don't start something we can't finish tonight, anyway your Mum and Dad are probably outside listening, I don't want to do anything that will upset them."

I giggle. "Yeah you're right," he pulls me in and kisses me and I can feel myself drifting away.

When I wake up in the morning I can feel Caleb behind me snuggling into me, I love waking up with him behind me. It just feels so natural, like it was always meant to be. I smile and wiggle my bum closer into him.

"Tasha you better stop that right now, I can just about deal with you being close to me, but I can't deal with you grinding against me."

"Sorry Caleb I couldn't help myself." I giggle again.

"That's it Tasha I'm getting up now, I really can't deal with giggly Tasha when we are under your Mum and Dad's roof." he laughs as he gets out of the bed. He puts his clothes on and stands at the door. "Are you coming down with me Angel or are you going to stay there giggling?"

"I'm coming with you." I say as I get out of the bed, I think I forgot I only had my panties on until I see his mouth drop open. "Oops sorry Caleb." I say trying to be coy.

He just laughs and waits until I'm dressed. We go down stairs together and Mum and Dad are in the kitchen. We have breakfast together and then Caleb says he has to go home because he has to go away for a couple of days and needs to tie up a few loose ends and pack for his time away. I walk him to the door and we hug and kiss like we will never see each other again.

"Caleb it's only a couple of days you know." I say touching his face with my hand.

"I know Angel, but I feel so close to you right now and don't want to leave you after yesterday." he kisses me on the mouth very gently.

"I love you Caleb and I am going to miss you so much."

"Me too Angel." I watch him walk to his car and drive off. I stand watching for a while and then I turn and go back into the house.

I spend the rest of the day negotiating with the estate agents on the house, they have an interested party and I want to push the sale through as quick as I can, I need to move on and find my own place. Caleb has some apartments he can rent me until I decide what I want to do.

26

I go to work on Monday and it's a really busy day and just before I leave I receive an email from Caleb's secretary, Suzie, asking me to attend a ball on Friday night as Caleb's partner. I have mixed feelings when I see this email, firstly I'm excited because I love dressing up and going to balls, secondly the last ball I went to was the one when Felix attacked me and thirdly I'm a little bit pissed that Caleb didn't invite me himself, but I guess he had his reasons. I reply and say that I would be delighted to go.

Caleb is still away on Wednesday and I arrange to leave the office early to meet Kammie so that she can help me pick a dress. We are not going drinking like we did the last time – that didn't end up well. We go to Cabot Circus Shopping Centre because they have some great shops and we can have dinner later when we found something. We went round lots of shops and eventually I tried on an emerald green dress in Ghost, it is slinky and sculpts my body. It is bias cut with a diagonal waistline which shows off my curves really well. The back is open to half way down my back with a bow at the base. It screams vintage style and I love it, I hope Caleb does too.

We stop at Café Rouge for dinner and we have a great chat about Felix, Caleb and Luca and not an alcoholic drink in sight.

I show my dress to Mum when I get home and she loves it, she thinks it will be beautiful. I'm so happy right now.

When I get into bed I text Caleb.

"I went shopping for a dress for the ball tonight, I hope you will like it, I love it"

"I love anything you wear Angel, you are beautiful in everything"

"You're just biased Caleb, but thank you ha ha"

"No I'm not biased you are beautiful inside and out. I've missed you this week, it's been really hard not to see you. I know we talk on the phone but it's just not the same"

"Me too, when will you be back? Can you

get back any sooner?"

"I won't be back until I collect you for the ball, I'm sorry Angel. I wish I could be there right now! I would kiss you all over and hug you so tight"

"I think I would do exactly the same to you Caleb, I miss you"

"I think it's time for me to go to bed Angel, I'll talk to you tomorrow. Love you xxxx"

"Me too xx"

I sleep well that night, but then I always sleep well since I've read Felix's note, he really did set me free.

Before I know it Friday is here and I am really excited about the ball and seeing Caleb, I feel a bit like Cinderella. I leave work at lunchtime and go and have my hair and makeup done and then drive home. I start to get ready and when I put my dress on I call Mum upstairs to help me zip it up. She comes into the room and she stops by the door. "Oh my baby girl you look so beautiful, even more beautiful than you did on your wedding day if that is ever possible." she comes over to me and gives me a gentle hug so as not to mess up my hair or make up.

"Thanks Mum that makes me so happy to hear, I feel beautiful, this dress is just so gorgeous. Do you think Caleb will like it? I feel like I'm going on my first date with him, it's so strange."

"He will love it Tasha, I don't know how he will be able to keep his hands off you." she says laughing.

"Mum," I shout. "Oh my god that is embarrassing." I laugh at her.

When she has finished doing my zip up we both hear the doorbell ring, it must be Caleb, my first instinct is to dive down the stairs into his arms, but one look from Mum stops me. "I'm going to go downstairs and open the door and when I call you then you can come down ok. Believe me it will be worth it."

She goes downstairs and I hear her talking to Caleb, then I hear her shout up the stairs. "Tasha are you ready, Caleb is here." I laugh to myself and walk to the top of the stairs, take a deep breath and start to walk down the stairs, slowly.

I can hear Caleb take a deep breath and then he says, "Wow, just wow." I smile, he says, "Tasha you look, you look amazing, like an Angel." he smiles a big smile that lights up his face.

"Well you don't look too bad yourself." I say because he looks hot in his tux.

He moves to stand at the bottom of the stairs and then takes my hand, he leans in and kisses me on the cheek and guides me out of the front door.

Mum says goodbye and I walk out to a limousine that Caleb has waiting for me, he holds the door while I get in and then he climbs in beside me, still holding my hand.

"Tasha can we just miss the ball and go back to my apartment, I've missed you so much and I just want to hold you tight."

"No Caleb, I spent a lot of money on this dress and I want you to show me off." I giggle.

We arrive at the ball and go in, I'm feeling nervous because I don't know these people, but Caleb makes me feel as if I belong, so my nerves quickly leave me. We have a great night, I met some lovely people and we danced and laughed for the night, it was perfect! Dillon and Meg are there, they make such a lovely couple. I really like her, we have become very good friends since I started working at Blue Eye. I told her about Felix the other day after I had read his letter, I feel like I can talk about it now.

27

When it is time to leave we catch a cab over to Caleb's apartment and we laugh in the lift, it was such a great night. When we get inside the apartment we go out onto the balcony, this is becoming one of my favourite places to stand and watch the world go by. Caleb always stands behind me and wraps his arms around me and pulls me in tight, I always feel safe here.

"Caleb, can we go to bed please, I want to feel closer to you than I do right now and that will only happen when we are in bed and you pull me close into you."

"I won't stop you if that's what you want." I turn and walk inside and Caleb follows me and then locks up, as I get to the bottom step I feel myself being lifted in the air and carried upstairs, I laugh and scream at the same time, Caleb is laughing. When we get into the bedroom, he puts me down on my feet and then he stands back to look at me. "You really do look like an Angel and I can't believe you're mine. Turn around so I can undo the zip please Tasha."

I do as he says and then when the fabric slips down my body I hear him gasp as he realises that I'm naked underneath and have been all night. "You're killing me Tasha. God I want you so bad." he comes up behind me and pulls me into a hug from behind.

"Caleb can I take your clothes off you?" I ask.

He answers gruffly. "If that's what you want then of course," so I take great pleasure in taking his tuxedo off because it doesn't matter how gorgeous he looks in his tux he looks even better without it.

When he is as naked as I am, I take his hand and pull him to the bed, then I stand in front of him and reach up and kiss him, he moans, I moan, then I gently push him on the bed. He looks at me with wide eyes, "Tasha only if you feel you're ready."

"I want to take control this time Caleb, I will know how far I can go. Are you ok with that?" I stand with my hand on my hips.

He chuckles, "God I'd love you to take control Angel." he smiles that beautiful smile.

I kneel down and pull him so his knees are bent and his legs are hanging off the bed, I want to take him in my mouth, I want to know I can still do this. So without waiting a beat I take hold of his cock and I lean until my mouth is hovering over it. I look up into his face and see that his mouth is open in anticipation and he has propped himself up by his elbows so he can watch my reactions.

I take the tip into my mouth and flick my tongue over the top to taste the pre cum on the tip, then I slowly move my mouth up and down and suck gently. Then I start moving my tongue round his cock and I take it out and look up, Caleb looks like he's in ecstasy. I do this for a while then I take my spare hand and cup his balls, I hear him groan again. I then take his cock out of my mouth and I lean down and take his balls into my mouth. When I've finished that I slowly kiss up his body, taking his nipples in my mouth and nipping them with my teeth. I hear Caleb laugh when I do this, I look at him and I can see he wants me and he wants control, but he promised me this one time.

I move further up so that I am straddling him and I lean forward and kiss him, deeply, I devour him and he devours me, then when he's not expecting it I lower myself down onto his cock, he cries out my name in my mouth. When I start to move my hips up and down he tried to move with me, I sit upright to stop him from doing that.

"This is my way Caleb, don't move!" he smiles.

"Do you realise how hard that is Tasha? You are the most amazing person I've ever met."

After a while I lean back and then I touch his balls with my hand, he closes his eyes, I can see he is getting close, I need some extra stimulation to get me off this first time, do I start to masturbate? "Caleb open your eyes please I want you to watch"

He opens his eyes and watches me rubbing my clit. "God Tasha I can't hold on much later. I'm going to make love to you later on but you are just so gorgeous sitting there that I just can't hold on."

I can't hold on either and as I'm rubbing I tip over the edge. "Caleb oh my god," and as my pussy muscles clench around his cock he soon follows me "Tasha" he shouts. I fall down on top of him, panting hard, then I feel him come out of me and he rolls me to my side, so that I am facing him.

"Tasha that was amazing, you are amazing, I love you so much." he says smiling and then leans over and kisses me.

"Caleb thanks for letting me take control, I needed to see how far I could go, I love you too." I say kissing him.

We lay wrapped around each other for a while, then Caleb says, "Do you want to go and have a shower to clean up?" I nod my head and he comes to my side of the bed and takes my hand and pulls me into the bathroom. He starts the shower and then he steps in, he pulls me in with him and he gently washes my face, then my body, then my hair. I do the same to him and then we step out and dry each other. We go back to the bed and climb in, we move to our natural positions with him lying behind me pulling me as close as he can get me. This is heaven!

The next morning when I wake up I can feel someone staring at me and when I open my eyes I see Caleb looking at me smiling.

"How long were you watching me sleep?" I ask drowsily.

"Only about 10 minutes, I like watching you sleep, you look so peaceful." he says leaning down to kiss me. "Now that you're awake Angel I want to make love to you and show you how I'm going to look after you forever." he kisses me on the nose and then rolls me on my back, "if you don't want me to go any further just tell me at any stage Angel, I will back off ok, but I know you are meant for me. I'm going to love you forever"

He certainly showed me how much he loves me, it was the most emotional thing I have ever done, he made sure I was ok at every stage and when he entered me I started to cry, he was upset and tried to pull out but I grabbed his ass and pushed him back in and told him they were happy tears because I didn't know sex could be this good.

A while later we got up and dressed and went to the kitchen for breakfast, it was when Caleb was making my coffee that he said, "Tasha we didn't use any protection are you on birth control?"

"I am yes, don't worry Caleb." I said smiling.

"I'm not worried. A child with you would be beautiful, I just didn't want you to start panicking that's all." he comes over and kisses me.

I tell him about the offer on my house and that I am looking for an apartment until I decide what I want to do. "Tasha move in with me, I know we've only known each other a few months, but I feel a connection with you that I've never felt before with anyone. You are my forever and I intend to keep you as close to me as I can." he leans down and devours my mouth.

I don't know what to say, I had wanted some independence, but now we've taken our relationship to the next level, I don't want to sleep in a bed without him, I need him!

"I'd love to move in with you Caleb as long as you're sure." I say looking up at him shyly.

He steps back and looks at me, he

smiles at me and moves closer, then he picks me up and swings me around. "You have made me so happy."

"I need to break it to my parents and then get my stuff together so can we say I'll move in next week?" I don't want to upset them and agree too quickly.

"I understand Tasha, next Saturday then and we can have a party to welcome you to your new home and I'll get my family to come too so they can meet you." he is grinning like a child and he looks so gorgeous.

I jump up and clamp my legs around his back and start kissing him with such passion, he pushes me back against the kitchen work surface and then he slowly undoes my clothes and when he has taken his trousers and boxers down he slowly enters me. Every time he pumps his cock into me he says a word, "I. Love. You. Natasha. You. Have. Made. Me. So. Happy." I can feel his breath getting faster and when he reaches down and rubs my clit I'm a goner and I start screaming his name. He quickly follows me and then he leans his head against mine and says, "Welcome to your new home Angel." and then he kisses me again.

28

We laze around for an hour or so and then I need to go home because I need to talk to Mum and Dad about moving in with Caleb. I don't know how that's going to go.

"Tasha I don't know if I can wait until next week for you to meet my parents. Will you come out to the beach house tomorrow and meet them? They're going to love you." he asks.

"Ok I'd love to meet them Caleb, I'll come over and meet them. I'll stay at home tonight with Mum and Dad and then I'll drive over about 12 tomorrow is that ok?" He comes over and kisses me.

"I'll miss you tonight, I can't believe how much I need you close to me. What did I ever do without you Tasha!" He hugs me tight, "Come on I'll take you home. I'm sure your Mum wants to know how the ball was last night." he smiles and wiggles his eyebrows.

I pinch him gently on the arm, "stop that," then I start laughing. Everything is so easy with Caleb, I can be me, Natasha, I don't have to do what he likes to make him happy. It's like a breath of fresh air.

We drive over to Mum's and then he walks me to the door. Mum opens the door as he leans in for a kiss. "Hey guys come on in and tell me all about the ball, I'm dying to hear, you too Caleb." she smiles at us.

Mum makes us coffee and we sit down and I tell her about the ball, the food, the dancing and most importantly the other dresses. I know that's what she interested in. After about an hour Caleb has to leave, I walk him to the door and we kiss goodbye. When I turn to go into the house, Mum comes over to me and hugs me. She whispers in my ear ,"I'm glad you managed to get past Felix baby girl, I can see it in your eyes," she chuckles.

I stand with my mouth open and then start laughing, she knows me too well.

I decide to sit down and tell them sooner, rather than later so that I can enjoy the rest of my weekend because I will only stress about upsetting them.

We walk in the kitchen and I go over and make coffee for all of us. "Can I talk to you about something?" I wave at the table for them to sit down. They both nod.

"I think it's time I move out again," I giggle. "There is an offer on the house and I know I can't go back there, so I'm going to take the offer. I was going to rent an apartment until I decided what to do. However, Caleb has asked me to move in with him." I look up and I'm surprised I don't see shock in their faces but two smiling faces looking at me. "I know we've not been going out for long and you might think it's too early, but it just feels right. We've been through so much, I've been through so much and Caleb has been there for me even when Felix was alive, he is my other half, Mum."

"Baby girl, you're right you have been through so much and you've become a different person because of it, I know that you wouldn't let anything like that happen to you again. Me and your Dad also know how much Caleb means to you, how he has helped you through this very difficult time. When we had to call him in the middle of the night to come and hold you and rock you because we couldn't help you, that was the night we knew how much you mean to him and how much you need him. Yes it is very soon, but I think because of what you went through your relationship has progressed very quickly. We can see how much Caleb loves you and how he will never let anything or anyone hurt you. We love him for that, you are precious to us and we can see how precious you are to him, so we understand why you want to move in with him and we are delighted." she gets up off the chair and comes over and kisses me on the head.

Dad smiles at me and takes my hand across the table. "You are my baby girl, Tasha, and it's very hard for me to let you go again after what happened to you, but I can see how Caleb looks after you and I'm happy for you."

"Thanks guys that means so much. I told him I wouldn't move in till next Saturday, to give me chance to sort the house out and my stuff that I have here. He wants me to meet his family tomorrow and then he wants to have a moving in party on Saturday night, which you are both invited to!"

We sit and talk about what I need to do with the house and all my stuff to get ready for moving out again.

I text Caleb after lunch to tell him that I have told my parents

"Hey Caleb, I told Mum and Dad and they were surprisingly happy"

"That's great, I told mine and they can't wait to meet you tomorrow. I'm missing you already"

"Me too, can't wait to see you tomorrow

xxx"

"I'll try to keep my hands to myself Angel, but I can't guarantee that I will ☺"

"Me too xx"

Kammie and Luca come to dinner and we sit around chatting and laughing and it feels great to be normal again. When I tell them I am moving in with Caleb, they are both delighted for me and hug me, they then tell me that they are moving in together too. It's such an exciting time and I'm so happy.

When they leave for the night I go up to bed and text Caleb.

"I'm going to bed now Caleb, will miss you snuggling up to me making me feel safe"

"I'll miss you snoring next to me ha ha"

"I don't snore, you do lol"

"I'm joking, I wish I could hold you in my arms tonight, I felt so close to you and then you went home. I think we will have fun making up time. Will you stay at the beach house tomorrow night with me? I'll make sure you get to work on time – honestly xxx"

"I'm sure you will lol, can't wait and yes I will stay with you tomorrow night, try and stop me xx"

"I love you Angel, so very much"

"I love you too Caleb, see you tomorrow xx"

"xxx"

I go to sleep with a smile on my face.

29

The next morning I wake up and feel a little nervous about meeting Caleb's family, but only because I want them to like me. I go downstairs and have breakfast with Mum and Dad and then I start to pack my things ready for my move next week, I know I won't be able to do much during the week with work and everything.

I drive over to the beach house about 12pm, I hope I'm there first because it will make it easier for me. I knock on the door and Caleb opens it within 2 knocks. He comes through the door and lifts me up so that my legs wrap around his waist and he kisses me like he hasn't seen me for a week. "I'd love that welcome every night Caleb." I laugh when he puts me down.

"I missed you Angel and if you want me to greet you like that then that's what I'll do." he laughs too.

"Am I late, are there people here already?" I ask looking around when we've stepped into the house.

"No they are coming about 1pm, I wanted to see you before they came because I didn't want to embarrass you when I did that." he kisses me again.

"OK so can I help you with lunch Caleb?" I ask as we walk into the kitchen.

"No it's all good, it will be ready just after they arrive," he takes my hand. "Come on lets go and sit on the decking for a while, here's a glass of wine seeing as you're staying the night." he hands me a drink with his other hand.

We walk out onto the decking and even though it is cold, it's beautiful, when I sit down Caleb hands me a blanket and I wrap it around me. We sit in silence for a while and then Caleb says, "You know Angel, this house is yours too, not just the apartment, I live in both during the week, so what you can see now, this is yours."

I sit with my mouth open, I hadn't thought about that, this house is beautiful and I could only have dreamed about living in a house like this, in a location like this, tears start to well up in my eyes as I take in all around me. "Caleb I didn't think about that, this is amazing, are you sure you want me to move in, to share this space with me?"

He comes over to me so quickly I didn't see him move, he kneels in front of me. "Tasha I love you and I want everything I have to be yours, all of this" he waves his hand at the sea, beach and then the house "is nothing to me without you in it. You make me appreciate all I have." he takes my hand and kisses it.

We hear a car pulling into the drive and so we go into the house, he takes my hand and we walk towards the front door. As we approach it the front door opens and a beautiful teenager comes into the house, "Caleb," she shouts running towards him, he doesn't let go of my hand as he hugs her with the other arm. "Addison you look beautiful, how are you?" he lets her go.

"I'm great Caleb, missed you the last time you were home, so good to see you." she says looking at me.

"Addison, this is my girlfriend Tasha," he says and I take her hand and shake it.

She looks at me and then takes me into a hug. "Any girl who can get Caleb to bring her to this house is a keeper in my eyes." she smiles at me.

"Addison I'm very pleased to meet you and if you want to tell me any embarrassing stories about Caleb then I'd be happy to listen to them."

She laughs so hard and then looks at Caleb, "I see why you love her." She walks off towards the lounge.

I look behind where she was standing and see an older couple watching our exchange, Caleb still doesn't let go of my hand while he goes over and kisses his Mum on the cheek, "Great to see you Mum and Dad you're looking better." he says hugging his Dad.

"Mum, Dad this is Tasha who I told you all about."

His Mum comes over and takes me into her arms. "Welcome to the family Tasha, if Caleb loves you then we all love you." she steps back.

I can feel a tear in my eye, "Thank you so much." I say.

"I'm Amelia," she says as she walks off.

His Dad steps forward and offers me his hand, "I'm Bill, it's great to meet you we've heard a lot about you." he shakes my hand and then joins the rest of the family in the lounge. I go and sit on the arm of the couch and Caleb gets everyone a drink. We talk about me moving in, about work and just general chit chat. When lunch is ready we move into the dining room and continue our talk in there.

Lunch is amazing as always, "Caleb where did you learn to cook like this?" I ask.

"He watched me cook for years and then would always come in and help me, so I showed him how I made the food." Amelia says.

"Well he learned very well, he always makes fantastic food, I'll be the size of a house if he continues cooking like that." I laugh and everyone laughs too.

We have a great afternoon, there was eating, drinking, talking and lots of laughing, but it is soon time for them to leave. Amelia and I tidied the dishes away and cleaned the kitchen up, even though Caleb is a great chef, he makes a lot of mess.

We walk them to the door and Amelia gives me a big hug. "So glad to meet you Tasha, we can't wait for the welcoming party next weekend," she turns and walks out the door.

"Tasha you make sure you keep Caleb in order, if he causes you any problems just give me a call." Addison says handing me her number.

I look at her and then I take her into a hug. "Thanks Addison."

Caleb's Dad is last to say goodbye, he takes my hand and shakes it. "It was really nice to meet you Tasha, I can see how happy you make my son. Thanks."

I smile at him. "He makes me really happy too." I look up at Caleb who is looking down at me and I smile.

"See you later Dad, I'll talk to you in the week and make sure you all come to the party next week."

We watch them climb into their car and drive off, Caleb closes the front door and then takes my hand and pulls me upstairs, "I never thought they would leave." he says as he pushes me gently onto the bed. "I've been dying to do this all day." he says as he lays down on top of me and kisses me passionately.

He slowly takes my clothes off and then stands back to look at me, "My Angel," is all he says as he takes his clothes off and then he pulls me to the edge of the bed and kneels in front of me, he kisses from my bellybutton down until he reaches my lips and then he slowly opens then with his tongue. He licks me until his tongue reaches my clit and then he slowly flicks his tongue over it, I groan and arch my back, he pushes my stomach back down onto the bed and then he pushes his tongue inside me, the pleasure is immense and before I know it I'm having an orgasm which is so powerful it makes me catch my breath.

When I start to get my breath back, Caleb slowly lifts me and moves me further up the bed. He kisses me and then starts to kiss down my body until he reaches my nipples, he knows how mad it makes me when he kisses my nipples, while I'm concentrating on the feelings he instills in me when he nips the tip of my nipple, he pushes his cock inside my already wet pussy.

"Oh my god that feels good Caleb," I moan at him, "give it to me hard, I want all of it, I want every bit of you, I want to know that I have every last inch inside me." I can't believe I just said that, he makes me so horny.

"Angel that is such a turn on when you talk dirty to me, tell me what you want me to do." he says pulling his cock out to the tip.

"Give it all to me Caleb, don't hold back, I need it hard and fast I can't wait anymore." I reach around him and put my hands on his ass, he slams his cock into me and I lift my hips to take more of him, I can feel my nails digging into his ass because I don't want him to take it out, he moves and pulls his cock out and slams it back in again a few more times, he then pulls out and flips me over onto my front, he then lifts my hips up to meet him and slams his cock in so hard I scream out, "Caleb."

He slams into me again, and again, and again and then finally I can't take anymore and I can feel my muscles tightening over his cock as my orgasm takes over my body, at the same time I can feel his cock growing as he erupts inside me.

When we have both finished we fall down onto the bed in a sweaty mess. I start laughing. "We couldn't even wait for them to get off the drive."

He laughs back at me, "I wanted to do that ever since you walked in the door this morning Angel."

We lay there getting our breath back and then decide to go for a shower because we were hot and sticky. We both go into the shower and clean each other up, then we get dressed and go downstairs.

It's getting chilly and Caleb puts the fire on, now this is perfect, what did I do to deserve this.

Caleb was true to his word the next morning he did get me to work on time. I was smiling all day remembering the weekend and how much I love him. On Wednesday Caleb had a meeting to go to and I went home to Mum and Dad for dinner. As I was driving up to the house, I saw Caleb's car in the drive, what is going on? My heart starts racing, maybe he doesn't want me to move in with him anymore, I can feel a panic attack coming on, but I won't let it consume me, he wouldn't do that to me.

I park the car and walk into the house, Caleb is sat at the kitchen table with Mum and Dad and they all turn to look at me when I walk in. Caleb rises from the table and comes over and kisses me and pulls a chair out for me to sit. So I do.

"Your Mum invited me to dinner Tasha, I was at my meeting and I wanted to see you so I came over, hope you don't mind." he smiles his amazing smile at me.

I let out the breath I was holding and smile. "Of course I don't mind, I like spending time in your company."

Dinner is good as always and we all chat very easily, Caleb is like a true member of this family and it's great to see Mum and Dad love him as much as I do. After dinner Caleb says, "Tasha will I take some of your stuff home in my car so you don't have so much to do at the weekend?"

"That's a great idea Caleb, come with me upstairs and I'll give you a couple of boxes." I get up from the table and take his hand, and we walk upstairs, when we get into my room, Caleb closes the door and then pushes me up against the wall and devours my mouth.

When he pulls away he says, "God I wanted to do that since I saw you, why do I always feel a need to devour you Tasha, you've got into my blood."

I smile at him and kiss him gently on the lips, "The feelings mutual Caleb."

We take a couple of boxes each and go

downstairs and put them into Caleb's car. "That means I only have a couple to bring on Saturday. Do you need me to do anything about the party?" I ask.

"No Tasha, you just need to move your stuff in on Friday night if possible and then the party starts on Saturday at 8pm." he smiles at me.

Then he kisses me goodnight and gets in his car and drives off. Me and Mum spend a couple of hours chatting about me moving in with Caleb and just general chit chat then its time for bed. I love chatting with Mum and I know I'll miss it, but I'll be able to see her whenever I want, not like when I was with Felix, he wouldn't let me go and see them without him. I see now he didn't believe I was just going to see them, his mind was telling him that I was going to cheat on him so he wanted to control where I went and with whom.

Life with Caleb will be so much better. I sleep peacefully again.

30

Before I know it it's Friday and I'm driving away from my parent's house with the last couple of boxes in my car. We had tears but they were happy tears and they are coming to the party tomorrow. I drive out to the beach house with my boxes and knock on the door, Caleb opens the door and laughs, "Tasha what are you doing, you don't need to knock this is your house too." he reaches out and kisses me before he goes to the car and takes my boxes out and brings them inside.

I unpack my clothes and a few bits and pieces to get me through the next few days, I have to decide how I'll split my stuff between here and the apartment. It will take a while to get used to it.

When we wake up on Saturday, Caleb says he has to go into town and did I want to take some of my stuff to the apartment. I said that was a good idea and we put some boxes into the boot of his car. He helps me to bring the boxes up to the apartment and then he says, "I've got to go out for a short while, then I will come back and we can go for some lunch if you want Tasha."

"Thanks Caleb, you sure you don't mind me putting all my stuff into your apartment." I ask.

Before I can finish the sentence he is at my side, "Tasha, this is your apartment as much as it is mine, remember that, what I have is yours." he kisses me hard on the mouth.

I nod, he leaves and I set about putting my few things around the apartment. It feels really strange to see my things on the side and in the cupboards but I'm sure I will get used to it. I walk into the lounge and onto the balcony. I stand looking at the view of the city and start to cry, this is mine, I have the most amazing man in my life and this is all mine.

I must have stood there for a long time, just taking in the view and watching the world go by because all of a sudden Caleb is behind me. "The view is beautiful isn't it?" he says.

I agree with him, "it's even more

beautiful with you in it too." he moves closer to me and puts his arms around my chest to pull me into him and kisses the side of my head. We stand like that for what seems like hours and then we turn and walk back inside the apartment.

"Come on Angel we have to go and get ready for the party," he smiles as he takes my hand and leads me to the lift to go to the car. Once we are in the car I try to ask him about the party, but he won't answer any of my questions he just keeps saying, "you'll see," at least I know when we get back to the house I will see for myself then. He keeps laughing at me and telling me I'm like a child at Christmas wanting to open my presents early. I laugh because that is exactly what I feel like.

When we get back to the house, I can't believe that he has had someone in to decorate the house for the party, there are balloons everywhere and I can see lots of food in the kitchen and wine glasses already laid out. I stare at him. "You did all this without me knowing?"

He smiles at me, "I did and more Angel."

We go upstairs to get ready for everyone coming and when we go downstairs it is 7.45pm and time for a drink, he pours me a glass of wine and we sit in silence taking it all in when the doorbell rings heralding our first visitors, we both stand and go to the front door, when Caleb opens it its Kammie and Luca. I run to them and hug the pair of them, Kammie can't wait to get in and look around, she pushes me out of the way. I laugh. "Come on I'll show you around, let's get you a drink first." she links arms with me and we go into the kitchen where I give them both a drink.

As I'm showing them around Amelia, Bill and Addison arrive and I introduce them to Kammie and Luca. Next to arrive are my Mum and Dad and we introduce them to Amelia and Bill. Addison has wandered off with Kammie and Luca to finish showing them around so that I can welcome our guests with Caleb.

Mum and Dad, Bill and Amelia move into the lounge with their drinks and sit down chatting. "Caleb I think they like each other." I say taking his arm and looking up at him.

He plants a kiss on my forehead. "Of course they do." Still more people arrive, there are friends from work and some of Caleb's friends from when he was younger, I look around and everyone looks so happy, it makes me smile. Dillon is here with Meg, they are a wonderful couple and they have had their ups and downs as well, but they love each other and they work well together. Caleb comes up behind me. "What are you smiling about Tasha?"

"I'm smiling because I'm happy Caleb, I never thought I could be this happy. Thank you for being there for me." I kiss him hard.

"Come with me Tasha" he says taking my hand and taking me into the lounge.

"Friends I want your attention please, I have something I want to say." Caleb says and everyone goes quiet.

"A lot of you know me and Tasha separately and some of you know both of us, well I am so happy Tasha agreed to move in with me, she makes me so happy. When I first met her she was going through something in her life that no one ever needs to be going through, yet through that time she became my Angel, the reason I have to breathe, the reason I was put on this earth to live. I hate being away from her and am delighted that she wants to be with me, I'm nothing special compared to her." I squeeze his hand. "Thank you all for coming along to this party I really appreciate it, but I have to say that I have lied to Tasha." I whip my hand out of his, he tries to grab it back but I won't let him, "I'm sorry Tasha I swore to myself that I would never lie to you, so I need to confess, this isn't a moving in party …." He takes a breath and I hold mine, then he kneels on the floor in front of me and takes my hand, I let him.

"Angel I can't breathe without you, I can't sleep without you near me, I don't ever want to be away from you, I want you in my life for the rest of mine. You are my everything Tasha, you are my forever. Will you marry me Natasha Phillips?"

Wow, I stand there with my mouth open just looking at him, but I can't see him as there are so many tears in my eyes. I nod my head as I don't trust myself to speak.

"Is that a yes Angel, I need to hear you say it." he says still on his knees.

"Yes, yes it is Caleb, yes I will marry you." he jumps up from the floor and puts a ring on my finger, it is only then I realise that he had a box in his hand, he lifts me up closer to him, I wrap my legs around his waist almost instinctively.

Before I know it everyone has a glass of champagne and are toasting us.

"To Caleb and Tasha, to their future." I smile as I look around, Mum and Dad are hugging and Mum is crying.

After kissing Caleb, when he put me down I wander over to Mum. "Are you ok Mum? Don't you want me to marry Caleb? Is it too soon?"

She pulls me into a hug. "No it's amazing the love that you two have. He came and asked Dad for your hand in marriage the other day, that's why he was there when you came home, so we kind of knew this was going to happen tonight, I didn't want to spoil the surprise. Me and your Dad are so happy baby girl, really we are." she kisses me on the head and when I stand back we smile at each other.

Kammie and Luca are next to congratulate me, "Yo bitch," Kammie says "you are one lucky lady." she laughs.

"He's one lucky guy." Luca says and Kammie slaps him on the arm "Ouch what was that for?" he asks.

"You shouldn't be looking at other girls like that." Kammie says.

I laugh and then they both laugh along with me. Amelia and Bill come and find me then and they both hug me and welcome me to their family, I'm so emotional I just want to cry but I don't, I hold it together.

After I have spoken to everyone in the room I walk out onto the decking for some peace and quiet and to reflect on everything that's happened tonight.

I hear the door open behind me and I assume its Caleb, but it's not, "Aren't you glad you took that chance now Tasha, aren't you glad you listened to me." it's Dillon.

I turn to look at him and then I walk over and hug him. "Thank you so much for believing in us, I will never forget what you did for us that night."

When I let him go he smiles at me and says, "I can see it was worth it for both of you. Good luck Tasha and you know where I am if you need to moan about him, I know his good sides and his bad sides." he laughs and I join in.

The door opens again and this time it is Caleb. "Are you trying to steal my girl Dillon?" he asks as the two of us are laughing.

"No mate, no one can do that, she belongs to you as much as you belong to her. Congratulations to both of you." he says as he turns and walks back into the house.

"Are you ok Angel?" Caleb asks as he takes me into my favourite position, with him stood behind me with his arms wrapped around my body and pulled in against his.

"Caleb, I love you so much I can't even begin to explain, you saved me more than once and I know that we belong to each other, you are truly my soulmate." he pulls me in even closer.

"I love you so much and I am so happy that you fell into my life like the broken angel that you were." he stands and rests his chin on my neck as we both stare out across the now blackened sea.

This is my life, this is my forever!

Epilogue

Six months later

Today is my wedding day and I'm so excited to be getting married to the man I love. This is the man who saved me when I needed saving the most. I love him with a passion I can only describe as overwhelming, I need him to breathe.

I'm in my wedding dress and my Dad is waiting for me. My Mum has just left my room after helping me into the dress, she was crying, but they were happy tears. I slowly walk down the stairs and see Dad at the bottom of the stairs, he looks so gorgeous in his tuxedo and he slowly looks up at me coming towards him, I think I can see tears in his eyes.

"Baby girl you look beautiful, I can't believe how gorgeous you look today, Caleb is a very lucky man and I will make sure I tell him so later." he says taking my hand as I reach the bottom.

Mum and Dad are both looking at me and I have something to say, I don't know how they will feel about this but I think I'd better just say it.

"Mum, Dad I need to ask you something, please don't be angry with me and I promise to tell Caleb later, but can we stop by Felix's grave on the way, I promise not to get my dress dirty. I just need to say goodbye." I ask holding in my tears.

"I think that is a lovely thing to do Tasha of course we don't mind." Mum says.

"Right, time to go if we are making a stop of the way." Dad says ever the punctual one.

We get into the car and drive to the graveyard. Mum helps me out and I lift my dress so it doesn't get dirty on the grass. I walk over to Felix's grave and I take a deep breath. "Felix, hi it's Tasha, I know you probably know that but I didn't know what else to say." I giggle he always knew I hated awkward moments, "I just wanted to thank you for setting me free and allowing me to love again. I won't forget the time we had together before the monster within you took over, I love you and I wanted to say goodbye." I sit in silence for a few minutes then walk back to the car. Dad is panicking thinking we will be late, but it's a brides prerogative isn't it?

When we arrive at the beach house Mum helps me out and then she goes inside. We had the beach house blessed so that we could get married here in our most favourite spot in the world. The ceremony is going to be carried out on the decking and then we will have a big meal and party inside, it is just our family and friends, the same group who were here when Caleb asked me to marry him.

Dad takes my arm and walks with me into the house, through the lounge (which has been cleared of furniture) and out onto the decking, all the time Dido "Thank you" is playing. As I'm getting closer to Caleb, I hold my breath I want him to turn around, to make me feel less nervous. As I think that he slowly turns and looks at me, he has tears in his eyes as he walks towards me. "I can't wait for you to get to the top," he says as he kisses me, "You look so beautiful Angel." he nods at my Dad and takes my arm and we walk to the altar together. The ceremony goes without a hitch and then when it's over he picks me up and carries me back down the aisle to the lounge. All I can hear is whooping and cheering, it is the happiest day of my life and it's not over yet.

When we are all seated for the dinner,

Caleb stands up and says, "we aren't really going to do speeches because they kind of ruin the dinner," everyone laughs, "but I just wanted to say that today will go down in my books as the happiest day of my life. When I saw Tasha coming down the aisle the sun was shining behind her and she looked just like the Angel that she is. Tasha you will always be my Angel." he bends down and kisses me. Then he sits down.

I stand up and everyone goes silent. "I know it's not customary for the bride to speak, but I never follow traditions." Everyone laughs because they know it's true. "I just wanted to thank everyone here for welcoming Caleb and I into your lives, for everything you have ever done to help both of us in our lives. Caleb, I love you more than anything in the world and I have a special gift for you today that I want you to share with everyone here."

Kammie brings over the box which has been expertly wrapped and has a shiny bow on the top. Caleb stands up. "What about my present to you Tasha, can I give you that now too?" he says smiling.

I nod, because I want to give him my present last. He smiles at me and hands me a small box, I open it gently and when I do I see a big platinum heart with a diamond encrusted key sticking out of it. "What's this for?" I ask.

"This is my heart and I'm giving you the

key to my heart Tasha." he smiles and then leans over and kisses me gently on the lips.

"Now it's your turn Caleb." I say handing him the box. He opens it really slowly and then I see his eyes open wide. He is speechless, he really doesn't know what to say. He turns to look at me and I nod my head "Yes" is all I need to say.

He moves closer to me and hugs me and kisses me, "You are so wonderful, this is the best present anyone could have given me Angel. I love you."

There are cheers from the crowd. "What is it? What is it?" Caleb looks at me for permission to show everyone, I blush and then nod my head.

He slowly takes the item out of the box and shows everyone it's a pregnancy test, it's positive. "We're having a baby," he says as he starts to cry. "We're having a baby." everyone cheers and people start coming up to congratulate us.

This is the perfect ending to the most perfect day!

This is the perfect beginning to the most perfect life!

The End

Acknowledgements

Once again a lot of people have helped me without even knowing that they have done so.

Again, my beta readers are troopers who help me on a daily basis and I wouldn't be known without my superstar pimpers! Thank you for believing in me. I hope you stay with me on my writing journey.

As always a big thank you to my family, facebook friends and especially my two voxer friends Meg and Natasha, who have helped me through any issues I needed help with – thank you xx

I also want to thank my family, friends and readers for buying my book and keeping my dream alive – I thank each and every one of you xx

About the Author

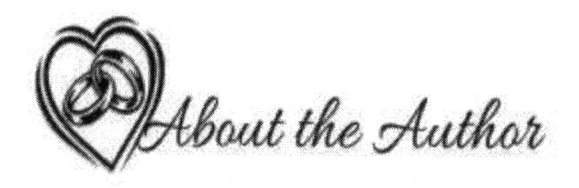

I think most of you have read this all before, so in the interest of not boring you, I'm going to change it.

This is the last book in the Til Death Us Do Part trilogy, however, it is not the last book in the series!

There are two more stories to be told:

Luca and Kammie's story – To Have and To Hold and
Dillon and Meg's story – For Richer or For Poorer

These will be released in the next couple of months so watch out for them.

After the Til Death Us Do Part series is finished, I have another couple of books which are currently "Work In Progress", so stay tuned to my facebook page: www.facebook.com/authorkrissy.vas for further details.

I love to hear what my readers have to say about my work so please find my links below:

Facebook:
https://www.facebook.com/authorkrissy.vas

Thank you for your support and I hope you enjoy this series of books as much as I enjoyed writing them.

Krissy V

TO LOVE AND TO CHERISH

Made in the USA
Charleston, SC
05 June 2014